UNSIGNED HYPE

a novel

BOOKER T. MATTISON

Revell

a division of Baker Publishing Group
Grand Rapids, Michigan

© 2009 by Booker T. Mattison

Published by Revell
a division of Baker Publishing Group
P.O. Box 6287, Grand Rapids, MI 49516-6287
www.revellbooks.com

Printed in the United States of America

Library of Congress Cataloging-in-Publication Data
Mattison, Booker T.
    Unsigned hype : a novel / Booker T. Mattison.
        p. cm.
    Summary: Fifteen-year-old Tory Tyson dreams of producing hip hop records, and as he rapidly begins to experience success doing just that, he finds that he must make choices between the way he has been raised by his single, God-fearing mother and the folks he meets in the music world.
    ISBN 978-0-8007-3380-3 (pbk.)
    1. Hip-hop—Fiction. 2. Rap (Music)—Fiction. 3. Conduct of life—Fiction. 4. Christian life—Fiction. 5. African Americans—Fiction. I. Title.
PZ7.M43545Un 2009
[Fic]—dc22   2008054966

10 11 12 13 14 15 16   9 8 7 6 5 4 3

Dedicated to Bump,
Mom, Chyance, Dog,
and Prep

1

Somebody's banging on my front door and it's rocking the house harder than the beat I'm laying down in my bedroom. If I didn't know better, I'd think the jump-out squad was knocking the door off the hinges with a battering ram.

When I peek through the peephole, I see Fat Mike bouncing around like he's about to wet his Red Monkey jean shorts. At eighteen, he's three years older than me, and if you saw him on the block, you'd swear Biggie had been born again.

"Open the door, son!"

When I do I get bum-rushed. Fat Mike is out of breath, and sweat drops pop off his forehead like a thousand little balled-up fists.

"They chose my demo, son!" he says, working hard to catch his breath. "And you know what else? Mixmaster Magic told me I had some banging beats!"

Now I'm officially floored.

For those of you who've been living under a rock for the past fifteen years, Mixmaster Magic is THE radio DJ in hip-hop on "the nation's number one station," Power 97. Not only is Mixmaster Magic a hip-hip pioneer, he's a hip-hop institution. Every rapper who's had a hit record in the last ten years has premiered their song on his show, *Magic Hour*, which is syndicated on 530 radio stations across the country and simulcast online.

"Yo, son. He said your beats sound like a cross between Pharrell, Swizz Beatz, and Just Blaze all rolled up in one! Round one is this Friday at 7 p.m.!"

I've never seen Fat Mike run before, but he's already gone. Now all I see is his back—and rolls of sweaty, jiggly flesh as he barrels up the block.

The 40 bus stops on the corner and burps a cloud of white smoke. My moms gets off and waves to Fat Mike just as he hits the boulevard and melts into the chocolate people parade.

Moms will be forty on her next birthday. She's not all secretive about her age like a lot of women because, according to her, "Each year you live is a blessing to be celebrated." That might be true, but I think it also has to do with the fact that she doesn't look a day over twenty-five. My friends always tell me how fine she is with her "mocha china-doll face" and "matching coffee-colored hair and eyes." It's my sonly duty to act offended, but as long as they're respectful my fuss is just a front because I know it's all true.

Moms is not even halfway in the house before I'm up in her grill like charcoal and cheeseburgers.

"Unsigned Hype picked Fat Mike's demo!"

She gives me that plastic, parade-float smile she uses only in family photos.

"Tory, that's great for your music, but you know how I feel about Power 97."

I didn't mention that Moms is real religious. She thinks you shouldn't listen to, watch, or read anything that goes against the Bible. Translation: don't entertain anything that could possibly be entertaining.

"Moms, a lot of hip-hop isn't supposed to be real. It's the rapper's imagination. No different from a movie or a video game."

Now why did I go and say that? She starts quoting Scripture, saying something about casting down imaginations and making thoughts obey Christ. Man, I wouldn't know how to do that even if I wanted to. Sometimes it's like she's speaking a foreign language. And I'm kind of disappointed because I thought she'd be happier for me.

She rubs my head and pulls me into a hug. "But I'll follow the competition as long as you're in it, because you're my modern-day Mozart and I love you."

I've never been a saint. The only saints I know are the names on churches and schools around my way, like St. Ursula, St. Peter, and St. Something on the abandoned building at the end of my block. I'm the youngest of three brothers, and I never knew my pops. He died when my moms was still pregnant with me. He was coming home late from work one night, and according to my moms it was a botched robbery attempt. They didn't get any money because my dad fought back. That part makes me feel proud, but in the end I guess he still lost.

My older brothers, Corey and Devin, say they remember him. They were three and two, so I guess they would.

Because I don't have any actual memories of my dad, I've created my own out of stories I've heard and pictures I've seen. In my mind these memories are as real as the ones that Corey and Devin have. I've always wondered if Dad really is somewhere looking down on us or if that's just something people say to create the illusion of an afterlife.

My moms is the executive assistant for a partner at Lufkin, Kravitz, and Klume, a law firm in New York City, so we have it better than most kids on my block. She found religion five years ago, and anytime I say that, she goes into this "it's not about religion, it's about relationship" thing. How can you have a relationship with somebody you've never seen? She actually talks to God like he's going to answer and calls him "Father" and really means it. She even told me he can be the father I never had. Okay, Moms. Right.

But I'm cool with the religious stuff because she doesn't yell as much anymore. It's only when she tries to push it on me that it becomes a problem. I still remember her drinking White Zin and going to the club with her girl-friends one Friday a month. Now she hangs out at church on days besides Sundays. And she won't even do the Harlem Shake when I play one of my beats for her. And *she's* the one who taught *me* how to Harlem Shake!

I'm in tenth grade now, but after school lets out next

month, I won't be going back. I'm dropping out because I know what I want to do with my life, and what they teach in school (if you want to call it teaching) isn't preparing me for my vocation. Geometry can't show me how to make music, and being in the school band is not going to get me a record deal.

I guess since I've been talking to you this long I should tell you my name. It's Tory Tyson. But I go by Terror Tory because I bring terror to all producers and DJs. And when I blow up (pun intended), I'm not taking sides, I'm taking over—terriTory, that is.

I've been into producing music since I was like ten years old. I started deejaying at friends' birthday parties in my neighborhood in Mount Vernon around the same time. Mount Vernon is a small city right outside of the Bronx. I mean small like 68,000 people.

My dad left behind a huge record collection. I'm talking hundreds of records. I have popular stuff and rare stuff with songs you can't get off "best of" CDs. I make more money when I spin at parties for older folks in their thirties and forties than I do at parties for people my age. So those old records do come in handy.

The older folks' parties I do are mostly for my moms's friends, which means they knew my dad. They're always telling me my DJ style is just like his was, and that I look just like him. It doesn't seem right that these people have actual memories of my dad and I don't. I wonder what the guy in the sky who made my moms a widow has to say about that.

But enough of the sentimental stuff.

11

My record collection is also where I get all the hot samples you hear in my beats. I'm ready to come out with my own record instead of spinning everybody else's. I've been saving all my money from my gigs so I can stop recording in the bedroom I share with my brothers and record a professional-sounding demo in a real studio. That's when I'll start sending my stuff around to record labels in the city.

Now I'm going to tell you why you should be glad you're getting to know me now instead of later. One day I'm going to produce songs for all the top hip-hop artists. That's where Fat Mike comes in. He's the best emcee in Mount Vernon, and he also works in the mail room at Power 97. I met him through my brother Devin's friend Cheryl—she's Fat Mike's sister. That's how I found out that Fat Mike was looking for beats. He became my first client when he paid me $100 to produce the three songs on his demo. I charged him another $7.25 an hour to record in my bedroom. I know, you're wondering how I came up with $7.25, right? That's minimum wage in New York. Talent fees can be negotiated, but studio time is never free. Fat Mike said that's what the rap stars say when they come through the station.

Because Fat Mike is always hanging out at Power, even on his days off, he knew about the Unsigned Hype demo contest before it was even announced on the air. The contest has three rounds, so if he wins, I win, because my music will be heard all over New York, New Jersey, and Connecticut at least three times. Even better than that, the winner gets a recording contract with Vantage Records, the hottest hip-hop label on the planet.

Fat Mike already told me that once he gets signed he wants me to produce everything he does. After that happens, all I need is one hit for my production fees to go through the roof. Then I can charge as much as $30,000 for each song I produce. So by the time I'm eighteen, I'll get a Lexus SUV. Then I'm getting out of Mount Vernon and buying me a crib in Harlem, where my dad used to teach. One thing my moms taught me is that we don't rent, we buy. Our two-bedroom house might not be the greatest, but it's ours.

Simply put, once I come out I'm going to be the man. Watch me. I have it all figured out.

My best friend, Boo Boo (I've known him since kindergarten and I still don't know his real name), just got home from juvenile detention last week. He was sent to Woodfield for six months for breaking all the windows out of our band teacher's F-150. We're the same age, but I feel a little older than him now because his life was on hold for half a year while I was learning a lot of things on the outside.

I'll let you in on a little secret. Boo Boo asked me to go with him the night he trashed Mr. Pisarcik's truck. I told him he was crazy. My moms is a lot nicer these days, but she'd still kill me for doing something like that. And to tell you the truth, even though Mr. Pisarcik is always giving me and Boo Boo detention, sometimes for no good reason, messing up his truck didn't seem like the right thing to do. A better way to get back at him would've been to take his loud, jingling key ring and lock him in the band room at the end of the day. It would've been awhile before anybody knew he was in there since he's usually the last one to leave school. And even when he got out, he wouldn't have been able to start his truck because he keeps all his keys on that same ring. But the best part would have been Mr. Pisarcik waiting for a tow truck in this part of town at night.

In case you couldn't tell by his last name, Mr. Pisarcik is white. And the only thing over here that would have looked like him at that time of night would be those spanking white cross trainers he wears with those colorful ties and striped shirts. Nothing would have happened to him, but I know he would've been spooked out of his mind, for real.

Since Boo Boo's been out, he's joined up with a group called the Young Warriors. Yancy and Carl, the two men who run the group, are in their twenties. They're into helping people my age stay out of trouble and off the streets. They're some pretty cool dudes, and not just because they bought and reopened the recreation center that's been closed down for as long as I can remember. They drive nice cars, but not all tricked out with rims and tinted windows. Yancy has an Accord, and Carl has a Camry. They dress nice too, usually a sports jacket and slacks and a crisply ironed shirt. No ties or pointy-toed shoes because that would be wack. Just some casual leather shoes they could rock with jeans if they had my style.

Wait, I haven't even told you my style yet. I'll start by telling you what it's not. I'm not into looking like no gangster (not that my moms would allow me to do that and live in her house anyway). But braids or stuff on my teeth? That's not me. Tattoos are also out. I can't see myself being a wrinkled old man explaining to my grand-kids why I have words and pictures painted all over me. Plus, how's the artwork going to look on a shriveled-up old body anyway?

I think some people would do anything no matter how crazy it looks, just because they've seen it on TV or in a magazine. Followers. That's something I'll never be.

But as far as my clothes go, I like jeans that fit me and a nice shirt. Like Kanye West or Jay-Z. They don't look all hard, but they still look cool. That's me in a nutshell.

In a short amount of time, Yancy and Carl have been able to get all kinds of people involved in the Young Warriors, from teenagers to schoolteachers. The first thing they put together was a community barbeque where ev-erybody helped remove the graffiti from the building. They'd heard about my DJ skills, so they hired me to do the music. They even paid me as good as the older folks do—$150 for the event. Another cool thing they started is a basketball league. Now most of my friends go up there after school to play ball. They're also planning on having block parties once school lets out, and they told me they want me to spin for those too. It's looking like it's going to be a good summer.

There's something else I wasn't going to tell you, but I might as well since I'm spilling half my guts anyway. I saw this fly young thing at the barbeque. She looked like a teenage version of Beyoncé, minus the tight clothes.

I'd never seen her before, and that's surprising because Mount Vernon is only four square miles. She didn't look at me or anything, but I still think she could like me if she actually saw me. I was trying everything to make her notice. I did my best scratching, mixing, and cross fading, but she wasn't moved by anything I did or played. Then she left before it was over. The next time I'll put on Jimmy Spicer's "Adventures of Super Rhymes." That's an old-school song that's thirteen minutes long. That should be enough time for me to introduce myself and get her number.

In school, the week leading up to Unsigned Hype is off the chains. The whole school has heard about the contest because everybody and their momma listens to Power 97 (well, everybody except my momma). People have heard that Fat Mike is going to be in it, but nobody knows that I made all of his beats. So I take it upon myself to anonymously leak that bit of information, because Moms says you should let other people praise you instead of you praising yourself. And the praise comes quick and thick.

A girl I don't even know corners me in front of the "Shhhh!" sign in the library. She sucks her teeth, puts her hand on her hip, cocks her head to the side, and whispers loudly, "So you're the one whose music is supposed to be on Power 97?"

I nod my head, and her face lights up like Times Square. She covers her mouth and unleashes a scream that crescendos. "That is tight—*tight*—TIGHT!"

Another guy asks me, "Those were your beats I heard on Fat Mike's demo?"

When I tell him they were, he removes his Yankees hat out of respect and covers his heart with it. He gives me a pound and shakes his head. "I got one word for you, my dude. Phat-tacular."

By the end of third period, the word on my beats has spread around the school like hot butter. And now it's on like popcorn. Even Mr. Pisarcik congratulates me. As he's talking, I can't help but stare at his key ring. I feel guilty for thinking about locking him in the band room.

Then at lunch, Gessie Johnson sits next to me. She's the prettiest girl at South Side High School, and she's only a sophomore. I feel like Biz Markie in that old-school song "The Vapors." People catch the vapors when they start acting different toward you once you make it. I haven't even done anything yet, and people are already catching it. So how are they going to act when I really blow up? Maybe that's why Gessie Johnson sitting next to me isn't as big a deal as I thought it would be. Or it could be because she *was* the prettiest girl in the whole world—but that was before I saw that girl at the barbeque.

Boo Boo, Fat Mike, and his sister Cheryl get to our house about six o'clock on Friday night. Corey and Devin are there too. They actually got off work early so we could listen to the competition together.

Corey and Devin both used to rap, but now they've moved on to other things. Corey's the oldest, and he's the math whiz. He graduates next month and already has a full scholarship to Norfolk State University down in Virginia, where my dad went to school. Devin wants to be the next Will Smith. He takes acting classes at the Play Group Theatre and played Othello in the Shakespeare play they did last year. He was really good. He had the language down and everything. He graduates next year and then plans to go to NYU to study acting. Corey and Devin go to Mount Vernon High School because it has better math and drama departments. I chose South Side because it's around the corner, so I can walk.

Moms got off work early, so by the time I got home from

Young Warriors, the house already smelled like a Chicken Hut. But Chicken Hut can't hold a candle to my moms's chicken fingers. She also made a banging spinach salad with Kalamata olives (my favorite) and homemade fries with the potato skins still on them. Of course Fat Mike eats more fingers and fries than all of us put together.

By the time everybody finishes eating, it's ten minutes to seven. Corey turns on the radio, and Slam Slade, the DJ whose show is before Mixmaster Magic's, is already talking about the competition. Fat Mike is going to be up against Big Numbers, a rapper from Brooklyn, and Capital and Flavorist Rhymes, two rappers from Queens. Wow. All three of those names sound hotter than Fat Mike, plus they're all from the city. I must be crazy to even think I can compete in something this big. I'm only fifteen.

My face must be saying what I'm thinking because Moms rubs my head and says, "You're going to do just fine." Nothing makes you feel better than your mother's real smile. Especially when your mother is as pretty as mine is. So if she says I'm going to do just fine, then that means I'm going to do just fine.

The whole house crowds around the radio. I look around and can't believe that something so important to me is this important to everybody else.

Fat Mike looks at me and grins, exposing his fake di-amond-and-platinum grill. He gives me a pound. "We about to get it done, son!"

After the commercial break, Mixmaster Magic shouts his famous show introduction through the radio, "New York! New Jersey! Connecticut! Stand up!" On cue, we all stand up (except Moms) and start getting light to the theme music for the show. Hearing Mixmaster Magic getting hype on the radio sends chills up my spine. I learned all of my early DJ tricks from listening to his show, and now the Magic Man himself is about to play a song I produced. That's crazy!

Flavorist Rhymes is first. His lyrics are tight, but his beats aren't really mixed right. I can tell they would sound better if they were recorded in a better situation. I feel bad for him, then I remind myself that this isn't a love fest.

Capital sounds like a younger version of Busta Rhymes. His beats are a little dated because he uses a lot of 808 kick drums and loose snares. But I have to admit the track is still kind of hot.

When Big Numbers comes on, everybody in the house (except Moms) starts bobbing their head. The song is hypnotic and has this catchy hook that goes, "Rougher than the toughest of the rough emcees. Tougher than the roughest of the tough emcees." I have to hand it to Big Numbers, that song is fire! But my confidence is growing now because we're going last, and I like our chances, depending on which track Magic chooses.

Before playing our song, Mixmaster Magic gives a disclaimer, which he didn't do for anybody else. He says, "I hope I don't bias the jury, but I have to say that this next artist has some of the bangin'est beats I've heard in a long time. But don't let that influence you, Tri-State. Everybody stand up for Fat Mike!"

We all go wild. Is it my imagination, or did Fat Mike

just cut me an envious eye? No way. I must be tripping. We're in this thing together.

Magic picks "Fly Girls I Attract." That's one of my favorite beats. In that one I sampled four bars of a Blackbyrds song from 1977 called "Mysterious Vibes." I slowed it down and looped it to give it a dark, street feel. Then I laid a knocking drum track underneath to pick up the tempo.

Remember when I told my moms earlier that a lot of hip-hop songs are the rapper's fantasy? Fat Mike's lyrics in "Fly Girls I Attract" are exactly what I was talking about. In that song he's supposed to be talking to a really attractive girl. The first verse goes like this:

> I caught you. Do you want to give me some play?
> I seen you spying on me. I seen you looking this
>   way.
> Now you front when I approach like you didn't
>   even see me.
> I know your man is wack, he couldn't measure up
>   to three me's.
> But you insist that I'm a player 'cuz I'm fairly at-
>   tractive.
> I tell you I'm a virgin, but you swear that I'm ac-
>   tive.
> Where's your evidence, baby?
> That's how rumors get started. Fly girls could
>   never play me.

Don't get me wrong, those lyrics are off the charts. But you have to see Fat Mike to understand why attracting

21

fly girls is pure fantasy for him. Not that I'm trying to play him or anything, because he's a cool dude and I like him a lot. But I don't think Fat Mike has even had a girlfriend before.

As soon as the song goes off, Magic comes back in with an excited, "Wooooooo! Every phone line is lit up!" He takes the first call. "This is Mixmaster Magic, who you voting for?"

The caller is a girl from Brooklyn, and she screams Fat Mike's name at the top of her lungs. Fat Mike's eyes get as big as quarters. His metal-mouthed grin stretches from ear to ear. The next call is a dude, and he goes on and on about how hot the track is. Magic finally has to cut him off to take the next vote.

Caller after caller picks "Fly Girls I Attract." It's not even close. I'm not going to lie, my head gets so big I'm surprised we don't have to renovate the house to fit it inside.

After the last vote comes in, Fat Mike's cell phone rings. He answers it and waves to Corey to turn the radio down. I can tell he's trying to be cool while he listens to the person on the other end. Then he passes the phone to me.

"Terror Tory? This is Mixmaster Magic."

My heart stops beating so I must be dead. I can't believe I'm on the phone with Mixmaster Magic!

"I wanted to call and congratulate you on winning the first round of the competition."

"Thanks a lot," I splutter.

"I'd like for you to come by the station on Monday around noon so we can talk shop and chop it up a bit."

Now I'm in dilemma central because Monday at twelve is smack-dab in the middle of the school day.

"Okay, that'll work," I say.

By the time I get off the phone, Fat Mike has slapped five with every hand in the house twice. Now all eyes are on me.

Moms speaks first. "What did he say?"

I look her in the eye and then around the room. "He told me congratulations."

"Is that all he said?" she asks.

Before I can even think about it, the lie jumps out of my mouth like it's wearing a pair of Jordans. "Yeah. That's all he said."

The room erupts into an all-out vicTory celebration. Moms even does the Harlem Shake.

◆

At 6:30 Sunday morning, Moms comes into my room telling me to rise and shine. I don't open my eyes right away, so she snuffs me with a pillow.

"You're going to church with me this morning," she says.

"You said when I turned fifteen I could decide for myself when I wanted to go," I shoot back.

Moms is having none of that. "You're going to church. Since you won that competition, your head can barely fit in this house. And arrogance is a disease that will cripple you if you don't watch it."

When we get to the church, I try to get Moms to sit in the back, but she's not having that either. "You don't have

23

to sit with me, Tory. You're a young man now. You can sit wherever you want to."

The loud preacher must have illegally wiretapped my brain, because his sermon is all about telling the truth. After fifteen minutes of his booming voice raining down on me like a hot-metal storm, I feel really guilty about lying. But what am I supposed to do, not meet with Mixmaster Magic?

I turn to check the clock to see how much longer the torture is going to last and find myself face-to-face with the girl from the barbeque. She's sitting in the pew right behind me, looking even prettier than I remember. She cocks her head to the side to see past my big head. Still not paying me any attention. I force myself to turn back around because she's sitting beside her moms and dad, and I don't want to be rude.

When the service ends, I take a deep breath to calm my nerves and stand. When I turn to introduce myself, she's already gone. I look around the church and see her and her parents about to head out the front door. Before they do, her parents wave to my moms on the other side of the church.

My heart feels like it's about to pop out of my chest as me and Moms walk to the bus stop. "You know those people you waved to after church?"

"Eddie and Barbara Lord? Of course."

She barely gets her answer out before I ask my next question.

"Did they just move here or something? I've never seen them before."

Moms sees that pitch coming and smacks it down to Yankee Stadium. "You haven't been here in almost a year, so why are you surprised?"

Okay, I see where this is going. I try the more direct approach.

"What school does their daughter go to?" I ask in the sweetest voice I can fake.

"She doesn't. Barbara teaches her at home."

"Isn't that illegal?" I ask, genuinely concerned.

"Of course not. It's called homeschooling." Moms stops in her tracks and asks the $100,000 question. "Why?"

My mind back flips into action at warp speed. Do I tell her I'm madly in love with this girl, or do I play it cool?

She's standing there waiting for an answer. Then a grin spreads across her face.

"You like her, don't you?"

"Well . . ."

Incredibly, the DJ who talks on microphones for hours at a time is tongue-tied. "Yeah, I guess so," I finish.

The grin leaves Moms's face as quickly as it came. "Don't even think about it, Tory. Unless your motive is friendship, your mind is in the wrong place." She starts walking again, but I can see that she's holding back a smile.

◆

On Monday I'm up at the crack of dawn. Corey and Devin are still out cold. Since it's three of us and only one of Moms, she gave us the biggest bedroom. That gives us the luxury of having a bathroom in our bedroom. This bathroom is also the vocal booth for my studio, so

25

whoever gets up first has to take the egg cartons off the wall. That way they don't get wet when the shower is turned on.

Even though Corey and Devin know these cartons are the soundproofing for my vocal booth, taking them down every morning sometimes gets on their nerves. They would never say that in a million years because they support me and my music so much. But I've heard the occasional sigh, and I've seen the tension wrinkles ripple across their foreheads on the mornings they're running late. Those actions speak louder than their words ever could. That's one of the reasons I hope something big happens at this meeting today. Maybe then I won't have to put them out so much.

After I get out of the shower, I quietly slip on my favorite outfit: a light tan Robert Talbott estate shirt, Paper Denim & Cloth blue jeans, and brown and tan Louis Vuitton Bastia Sneakers. I take a long look at myself in the mirror. Yeah, I definitely look fifteen. Not much I can do about that. My sigh sounds like a shout since the house is so quiet.

I peek out of the bathroom and see that Corey and Devin still haven't moved a muscle. I dip into Moms's bathroom, which is just off the main hallway of the house. I rummage through her makeup drawer as quietly as my nervous hands will allow. As I'm doing this, my forehead starts itching. I feel up there to make sure there's not a big "L" for "liar" stamped there. Fortunately, it's not.

After sorting through hundreds of compacts and containers, I hit the jackpot. With no time to waste, I carefully manufacture hair over my top lip with Moms's eyebrow pencil.

When I'm done, I pucker up and rotate my lips to see how the mustache looks when light hits it. Hmmm, looks like the 'stache is a little crooked. I draw more hair on the right side to make it even with the left. I look again. Too much. If I keep this up, I'm going to look like Rick Ross. I wipe it off and scrap the whole idea.

Just as I'm putting the pencil back in the drawer, Moms appears.

"Tory, what are you doing?"

There's a nine-month pregnant pause. I curl my lips in and pop them together, sneaking a couple words through each time my mouth opens.

"My lips . . . are mad . . . crusty."

Moms produces a tube of lip balm. Does she sleep with this stuff or something?

I reach for the tube. She slaps my hand away.

"You always use too much."

She grips my head, applies a thin layer of lip balm, and then closely examines the fruit of her labor. "They don't look chapped to me."

"Just keeping them moist, Moms. Just keeping them moist. Thank you, though."

"You're welcome." She stares at me long and hard.

Oh snap, she must've sniffed me out. I don't know about your moms, but mine has superpowers. She figures out stuff that normal people can't without surveillance equipment. Now I'll have to come up with another lie to cover up the first two.

"The older you get, the more you look like your dad," she says.

That familiar look of pain returns to her eyes. It's always made me sad to see her look like that because I know she's thinking about Dad dying.

When I was younger, I would get my toy piano and play all of my scales for her to take her mind off it. Now that I'm older, I realize that probably made her think about him more because she's always said I inherited my love of music from him. Knowing that and wanting to take her pain away is what motivated me to be more than just a good piano player. My goal was to compose great music like Beethoven, except I wanted my compositions to be flavored by the streets. Of course, my old English piano teacher couldn't understand why his most gifted pupil would "squander his talent producing popular poppy-cock," but Moms supported me, and that's all that mattered.

Moms rubs my head. "You're growing up to be a fine young man." She smiles as she says it.

If only she knew.

A cab to 241st Street in the Bronx takes three minutes from our house. Walking would take eight, so I cab it. 241st Street is the last stop on the 2 train. I'll take the 2 all the way down to Times Square, where Power 97 is located.

Before I go inside the train station, I stop in front of Peppino's. This is the spot where my dad got killed. He was on his way home from tutoring one of his students in Harlem, where he taught fifth grade math. Anytime he worked late, he would stop by Peppino's and pick up a large pie with pepperoni and extra cheese. That was some kind of romantic ritual Moms and Dad had to "keep the flame in the fire," as she puts it. She says that my dad would tell Corey, Devin, and even me inside the womb, "If it wasn't for pepperoni pizza, none of you would be here."

According to legend, the two of them met at a pizza parlor where the oven broke down right before they each came in. There was one slice of pepperoni pizza left, and they both called for it at the same time. Dad was a gentle-man, so he let Moms have it. She was impressed with this "chivalrous act," so she told him she'd split it with him. Dad, still being a gentleman and trying to impress her as a big spender, said he'd pay for it *and* add extra cheese. When he took the slice to her table to cut it in half with one of those white plastic knives, she invited him to sit down. And the rest, as they say, is history.

Moms makes this into a moral tale. She says that she gave half of all she had and still came away with more than enough. Not just physically from the food, but emo-tionally from a good man who became her husband. She always ends the story by saying, "Give and it shall be given to you. Pressed down, shaken together, and run-ning over."

On the night he died, Dad got jumped from behind by two guys as soon as he came out of Peppino's. Sup-posedly nobody saw anything. I know better because it was seven at night and people are out here 24-7. But I know the deal. In the hood, not snitching is some stupid badge of honor.

So people like me who lose their dads don't matter? Or is it no big deal when someone loses their dad, because so many people in neighborhoods like this don't have dads themselves? But that can't be true, because it's not just dads dying. It's sons, brothers, cousins, uncles, daughters, sisters, mothers, aunts, and best friends. Did it ever occur to people who see crimes happen but don't say anything that it only makes the streets they live on more dangerous?

I angrily wipe the tears off my face and suck it up. I can't let anybody see me being soft.

Anytime I catch the train at 241st, I stand just inside the door of the subway car. When the doors close I see my reflection in the glass, and it *is* just like looking at my dad. I wonder how many times he thought about me, Corey, Devin, and Moms as he took this same train to and from work every day. He wouldn't be happy about me lying to Moms, but I'm sure he'd be proud of me trying to make my mark in the world by deejaying and making music. I wonder if he ever thought about deejaying professionally. I've heard that he was really good, but he only did it for friends and family and sometimes for events at his school.

When I go to the city, it's always the same thing. Stop by Peppino's. Pay my respects. Get angry. Get on the train. But slowly thoughts of my dad are always absorbed into the excitement of riding the subway through the Boogie Down Bronx. This is where hip-hop was born.

I shift my focus from my reflection to the rugged Bronx terrain as it whizzes by. I imagine Kool DJ Herc, Grand Wizard Theodore, Afrika Bambaataa, and Grandmaster Flash carrying DJ equipment and crates of records to block parties on these same streets. I put my earbuds in and play my latest beats to provide a sound track to my imagination and to connect myself with this history. This trip is extra special, though, because I'm going to Power 97 to meet with Mixmaster Magic. Deep in my soul I feel like life after today is never going to be the same.

I don't sit until the train goes underground at 149th and 3rd Avenue.

Power 97 takes up two whole floors at One Times Square. The business offices are on nine and the studios are on seven. You can afford that much New York real estate when you're the number one radio station in the whole universe.

I'm so starry-eyed when I walk in the building that I almost float right past the doorman.

"Hey!" he calls out. "You're dressed too nice to be a delivery boy, and you're too young to be in here during school hours. Where do you think you're going?"

I come crashing back to earth, embarrassed and slightly intimidated. But I'm not going to let some doorman punk me in public.

"I have an appointment with Mixmaster Magic," I fire back. He studies me like a math problem before picking up the phone. This guy must have eyes on the side of his head because he's still able to wave people through the electronic sensor without taking his eyes off me.

"You have ID?" he growls.

I whip out my South Side High School identification card, the one with the picture of me when I was a fourteen-year-old freshman. No doubt my tough-guy front is undone by my naked top lip and skinny frame.

He hangs up the phone with authority. "Nine."

"Thank you," I say, glowing on the inside but still maintaining the ice grill.

I walk toward the sensor but not before the doorman's

long arm comes down to stop me. He stabs a meaty index finger into a book on his desk. "Sign in!"

When I get to the ninth floor, I'm surprised. The business offices look as corporate as my moms's law firm. I thought the station would be as hip and cool as the music they play.

When I round the corner, I see the biggest difference between Power 97 and Lufkin, Kravitz, and Klume. The receptionist. She looks like she's straight out of a music video. Women in Mount Vernon just aren't built like that.

As I approach the desk, she flashes a perfect smile that shows off perfect teeth. My eyes get big because she has truly taken my breath away.

"Hiiii," she says. "What can I do for you today?"

It takes me a second to respond as I scramble to get my cool together. It's not happening. "I have an appointment to see Mixmaster Magic," I stammer.

She wrinkles the bridge of her perfect nose and sighs. "Teenagers today. Cunning little creatures you are. Let's do this. I'll give you an autographed picture since you were sharp enough to get past the doorman. But it won't be possible for you to meet Mixmaster Magic."

She thinks I'm playing. And do I detect a patronizing tone? She's quickly sinking to the level of the doorman.

With shoulders squared and chin held high, I proclaim, "Tell Mixmaster Magic that Terror Tory is here!"

She raises her perfect eyebrows, but her attitude does change from annoying older sibling to serious. She picks

33

up the phone. "Hiiii. A Terror Tory is here to see you?" She listens and then hangs up. "Seventh floor, he'll meet you in the lobby."

I bounce. When I glance back, she's staring at me with a look of complete shock.

I hear hip-hop music playing before the elevator doors even open on seven. When I step off, I'm serenaded by the hook from Nas's hip-hop classic "The World Is Yours":

> Whose world is this?
> The world is yours.

I can't help but think this is a sign.

The seventh floor is very different from nine. This must be what an upscale nightclub looks like: mood lighting, modern decor made up of oddly shaped glass tables and dark-colored, high-backed seating that would swallow up a grown man like a midget. This is what I imagined a radio station like Power 97 would be like.

Standing in the middle of the lobby is a large man with expensive-looking glasses and a beard so perfectly trimmed it could've been drawn on with Moms's eyebrow pencil. Could this be the Magic Man?

He looks as surprised as I am when he sees me. "Terror Tory?"

When I hear that golden voice, I know it's him. For some reason the people with the smoothest voices never look as cool as they sound. If I had to describe Mixmaster Magic, I would say he looks like a hip-hop Santa Claus, but not nearly as old.

I extend my hand to shake. He pumps it and says, "I

thought you sounded a little young on the phone. What are you, like fifteen?"

"Sixteen on the Fourth of July," I say.

Magic shakes his head. "I have to apologize, man. If I knew you were that young, I would've talked to your mom before arranging a meeting with you. And I definitely wouldn't have had you come out here during school hours. Aren't you supposed to be in school right now?"

"I'm dropping out," I say, praying that my golden opportunity isn't slipping away before my eyes.

"Dropping out?" He turns and motions for me to follow him. "Step into my office."

We pass another music video receptionist as we walk down a hallway lined with framed gold and platinum records autographed by everyone from OutKast to Kurtis Blow. When we get into his office, I'm in awe. He has original flyers covering his wall from parties at classic hip-hop spots like the Latin Quarter, the Rooftop, Union Square, and the Skate Key. And to top it off, he has a flyer for the party where the famous battle between Kool Moe Dee and Busy Bee took place in 1981.

"You were there?"

"Eleven years old," he says. "That's when I knew I wanted to be a DJ. Of course, my mom beat the skin off my butt for coming home so late. But swollen cheeks is a small price to pay for witnessing history." He turns serious. "So what makes you think dropping out of school is the right thing to do?"

Without even thinking, I blurt out, "Jay-Z, Biggie, 50. They all dropped out, and look at them."

Magic responds, "Chuck D from Public Enemy, Russell Simmons, P. Diddy, and me."

"You what?"

"Everybody I named finished high school *and* went to college. So you need to get back to school right now before I get thrown in jail for making you a truant."

"School lets out for the summer in two weeks," I say, willing to try anything to keep from getting sent home.

"Well, come see me in two weeks."

Dejected, I get up and slowly head for the door.

"One question," Magic says.

I turn around, hopeful. I can tell he's trying to figure something out. "How does somebody fifteen know about the Blackbyrds and 'Mysterious Vibes'?"

Now he's speaking my language, so I launch. "I spin too. I have 823 records in my collection. And 137 are from the 1970s."

"You spin too?"

"All the time." My hand is still on the doorknob.

"What jam would you play to keep the floor hopping if the crowd was half young heads and half old-school?"

"Frankie Beverly and Maze, 'Before I Let Go,'" I say quickly.

"How long would you keep it on?"

"Two minutes forty-three seconds until right after the guitar solo. On the drum lick at two forty-five, I'd bring in Mario's 'Let Me Love You.'"

Magic seems to be playing it out in his head. "Frankie Beverly to Mario. I never would have thought about that one. You've done that at a party before?"

"No doubt!" I say. "But that's not the knockout blow. After I let Mario run for two thirteen, I bring in Lupe Fiasco's 'Superstar.' That's when the whole crowd goes wild."

Magic seems to be hearing the music and seeing the dance floor in his mind. He nods and smiles.

"I'll see you in two weeks. And when you come back, have me seven or eight beats to listen to. I've wanted to get new music for my show introduction for the last couple of years. When I heard your tracks, I knew you had the sound I was looking for. It's the perfect combination of the old and the new. That's the kind of feel I want to bring to my show now."

Mixmaster Magic has been using the same music for his show intro for as long as I can remember. It's a New York institution. I don't trust what I'm hearing, so I make sure. "So you want *me* to make some beats for *you* for your show introduction?"

"Yeah," he says. "And don't worry, I'm going to pay you. Fat Mike tells me you drive a hard bargain. Leave your contact information with the receptionist."

When I step out of One Times Square, I look up 7th Avenue and Broadway. The flashing lights are brighter, the images on the video screens are more alive, and the people and traffic are buzzing with the same energy I feel in my chest. I take a deep breath of New York City before I head underground to the train.

4

When I get to school on Tuesday, Boo Boo is outside waiting for me. He looks impatient.

"Where were you yesterday?" he demands. "The whole school was looking for you, including Gessie Johnson." He nudges me for emphasis on that last point. "I didn't know where you were, so I took advantage of some of your shine myself." He slides a crumpled piece of paper into my hand. I open it. Gessie's phone number is scribbled on it in Boo Boo's handwriting. "When I asked her for her number, she said she'd only give it to me if I gave it to you."

All of a sudden I'm surrounded. Everybody is congratulating me on winning the first round of the competition. I just want to get in the building and get to class. But it doesn't seem right not to at least look like I'm grateful for the support. One guy says he wants me to make him some beats. Another guy starts rapping in my ear. In my other ear a dude starts doing the human beat box. I'm getting hit with spit from the beat box guy, and his breath is kicking like feet.

Suddenly the sea of people parts, and Gessie Johnson waltzes through like a princess at the ball. It seems like the whole world goes silent, street traffic and all.

"Hi, Tory," she says.

"Hi," I respond.

"I gave Boo Boo my number to give to you."

I hold up the wrinkled piece of paper. "I have it right here."

"You can call me up to seven o'clock. I can't get calls after that."

"Okay."

"Bye." She dances off as royally as she came.

That was weird. My moms always tells me that a man who finds a wife finds a good thing. And she makes sure to emphasize the part about the man finding the woman, not the other way around. I guess that's her way of protecting her three sons from what she calls "fast women." Besides, Gessie didn't even know I existed until last week. Do I look different now or something? The fact that she wants me to call her just because I'm in some competition makes her lose a few points. It's cool she gave me her number, but what happens if somebody like Bow Wow shows up? Is she going to kick me to the curb because he's famous and I'm not (at least not yet)?

I shake my head and head inside.

By the time I get to homeroom, I've said thanks about a thousand times. Congratulations, big ups, and shout-outs are great, but does everybody in the school have to give me one?

Well . . . let me think about this for a minute. This is probably what life's going to be like once I'm famous. And since school lets out in two weeks and I'm not coming back after that, I might as well just enjoy it.

The attention becomes a lot less annoying now that I've decided to soak it all up and just *be*. Have you ever seen those Spike Lee movies when he sits the actor on the camera and it looks like they're floating through the scene? That's how I feel when I'm walking down the hallway now. Out of the corner of my eye, I see the stares. Then a smiling face pops up right in front of me. I give a pound, slap five, give a hug, smile, and keep floating.

I collect a few new clients too, but I'm torn. I'm not sure I want to sell my beats to people who have the money but no talent and no chance of making it. Money is important, but now that I'm making power moves, I have to start thinking about how I want to position my music. I'm sure Danja doesn't sell his beats to just anybody, so why should I?

I meet Fat Mike after school, and we head over to my house to work on some new songs. Right now I'm not charging him for the beats since we're working on his album. I'll get paid by the label once he gets signed. I do still charge him the $7.25 an hour for studio time, though.

I asked Moms to find out from her boss, Mr. Lufkin, if delayed payment was okay since I haven't asked Fat Mike to sign a contract. Mr. Lufkin thinks it's no big deal because a major label like Vantage Records would never release a song before they made sure the music was paid for, especially when the tracks have samples that need to be cleared. He did say that a smart business-man negotiates his exit strategy before he even begins a partnership. According to him, you always get better terms of separation in the beginning of a relationship before it sours. He thinks I should be more concerned if Fat Mike never gets a record deal or if we have a falling out. If Fat Mike continues to use my tracks to generate income or publicity for himself after that, Mr. Lufkin says I should be "duly compensated for my contribution to Fat Mike's monetary gains."

I think he's right, but me and Fat Mike are friends, so we don't have to worry about that. Plus, not winning isn't even an option. We destroyed the competition in the first round. We already have this thing sewed up.

Fat Mike is totally consumed with all the props he's been getting. "Yo, son. Everybody is sweating me now!"

I brace myself because I've been around him long enough to know when the fairy tales are about to begin. He thinks that because I'm three years younger than him, he can tell me anything and I'll believe it. I might not be the sharpest pencil in the box, but I *am* in the box.

"Every girl I see is trying to get at me now. AAAAHHHH!" he shouts at the top of his lungs.

He does that a lot. I call it the superhero shout. He could be in the middle of your grandmother's funeral, and if he got excited he'd still do it. It's like he can't control it.

The first couple of times he did it, I almost jumped out of my skin, but he doesn't get me as much anymore.

He pounds his chest like Kevin Garnett and breaks into the hook of "Fly Girls I Attract."

> It's always the fly girls I attract.
> As for looks, I get a compliment from girls each day.

He slaps me five so hard my palm burns. I hate it when he does that. He does the same thing when I play a new beat for him that he likes. I guess if he thinks something's hot, he makes your hand hot in return. Then he shouts about it.

"You know the first thing I'm gonna buy when I sign this deal, son?"

I don't realize he actually wants me to answer until he gives me a chunky elbow to the ribs.

"No," I gasp.

"A stick."

"A stick?"

"To beat off all the girls who're gonna want me after my album drops," he states. "But for the fly ones—no sticks, just chocolate kisses from the man himself!"

Uh-oh, he's referring to himself in the third person.

I can see that he's still cheesing and looking at me, so I look back and give him a nod. "Sounds cool."

He sucks his teeth. "Watch."

When we get to my block, we see a tricked-out Escalade parked in front of my house. It's all black and sitting on thirty-inch chrome Mogul DUBs.

"Looks like you got royalty at your crib, son!" Fat Mike says.

We get up close to check out the interior of the vehicle, but the windows are so tinted that all we can see are our dumbstruck faces staring back at us. We check the license plate. It says MAGIC MAN.

"Yo, that's Mixmaster Magic! He's at your house, son?"

"I don't know," I say, hoping my voice isn't shaking. I feel the cold sensation of fear wash over me like water over a levee in the 9th ward of New Orleans.

As soon as I get in the living room, I know I'm in big trouble. Moms is sitting on the couch with her arms crossed. She only crosses her arms like that when she's trying to keep rage from jumping out of her chest. Her and Mixmaster Magic look up at me and Fat Mike at the same time. Moms's eyes squint and get close together. That's the look me, Corey, and Devin call "the eye of the storm," and she's giving it to me something awful right now.

"Tory, get your narrow hips over here," she says. Then she makes a seamless transition to honey roses and smiles. "How are you, Fat Mike? Tory's in a world of trouble, so he's going to have to see you later."

"I'm doing fine, Mrs. Tyson. What up, Mixmaster? Tory, get at me later." Fat Mike backs out of the house with his thumb to his ear and his pinky to his mouth. "Call me," he mouths.

I sit in the chair just inside the entrance to the living room. "I said get over *here*," Moms snaps. I move to take a seat beside her on the couch.

Magic looks at me and says, "What's happening, little man?"

"Other than planning my funeral after you leave?"

Magic looks at my moms. "Should I go first, or do you want to?"

Moms gives me the iciest grill I've ever seen. "On Friday night, you didn't tell me that Mr. Magic—"

"You can call me Fauntleroy," Magic interrupts.

"You didn't tell me that Mr. Fauntleroy made an appointment with you. And you definitely didn't tell me the appointment was during school hours. You said the only thing he told you was congratulations."

I don't know if she wants me to answer since technically she didn't ask me a question. After a moment of her not taking her eyes off me, I figure I have to say something, so I try, "Yes."

"Yes what?" she demands.

Now I'm really confused. "Yes, ma'am?"

"Tory, you better stop playing with me."

Magic butts in and saves me from what surely would have been a clean shot to the head.

"Tory, listen. I came here to apologize to your mother because I didn't find out how old you were before I told you to come by the station. I blew it. I accept that. Your mother is understandably upset because she didn't know you cut class, and she definitely didn't know you were planning on dropping out of school."

Dude ratted me out? I go from being scared to being heated.

Magic turns his attention from me to Moms. "Mrs.

Tyson, I agree that Tory should be punished. But I think pulling him from the competition would be a bad move for two reasons. One, that won't punish just him, it will also punish Fat Mike, and he had nothing to do with it. Two, I've helped build the careers of some of the biggest names in the industry, and I know talent when I see it. Your son has a gift."

She's trying to pull me from the competition? If she does that, I don't know what I'm going to do, but I'm going to do something.

Moms has never been one to let other people make her decisions, so I'm sure she isn't going to let Mixmaster Magic know how she's going to play her hand.

"I thank you for coming by, Mr. Fauntleroy, but you should be—"

"Actually, if you're going to call me mister, my last name is Wiggins."

"Mr. Wiggins, you should be ashamed of yourself. What if something would have happened to Tory when he was down in the city and I thought he was at school?"

"I have nothing to say in my defense because what I did was indefensible. I just hope this isn't the way my relationship with your family ends."

Magic gets up and heads for the door. Moms escorts him out. He turns to me and says, "Little man, listen to your mother. She's a good one."

My punishment is that I can't leave the house, talk on the phone, or have any contact with the outside world for a whole month except at school. I also can't work on any beats because Moms locks all of my equipment and records in the closet in her bedroom. She even makes me take the egg cartons off the wall in the bathroom. Corey and Devin will get ready a whole lot quicker in the morning now.

Moms was going to let me get a cell phone for my birthday, but that's out now because she doesn't think she can trust me. At school I get joked all the time because I don't have a cell phone. Ten-year-olds have cell phones these days. But none of that matters to my moms. She thinks cell phones just give people my age another way to do sneaky things their parents can't find out about. Of course my cooked-up scheme only proves her point.

But I'm cool with the punishment because she doesn't make me drop out of the competition. I hope Mixmaster Magic still wants me to make some beats for his show introduction. He wanted them in two weeks, but I won't be able to give him anything for at least a month. Then I'll have to snail mail him a CD because I've been banned from going to the city. And that ban is "indefinite," so I don't know when I'll be going back again. If we had a computer in the house, I could email him the tracks after my punishment is over, but we don't. Actually, we do, but that computer is so old it's on life support. The only thing it's good for is word processing, so forget about the Internet.

I look at the calendar on the wall and see that I'm going to be on punishment when the Young Warriors' first summer barbeque jumps off the Friday after school lets out. That's $150 *and* mad fun down the drain.

I'm in my bed staring at the ceiling, trying to figure out

how to clean up the mess I made, when Moms comes in. She sits on the edge of my bed, and I notice that her eyes are red. She's been crying.

"It would be easy for me to come in here and yell and scream at you for thinking about dropping out of school. But I'm not going to do that. I want you to explain to me why you think dropping out of school makes sense."

Since the cat's already out of the bag, I might as well come clean. "I want to make music, Moms. And I'm good at it. You heard what Mixmaster Magic said. Besides, most people who are successful in this industry dropped out anyway. It's like basketball. Nobody needs college anymore. There's too much money to be made in the NBA . . ."

My voice trails off because I know my words are only piling on to her pain. She takes a moment to respond, but when she looks up, she's more serious that I've ever seen her.

"Do you realize that 150 years ago, it would have been illegal for you to learn how to read in this country?"

"I've never really thought about it," I confess.

"And what do you think your grandparents, your great-grandparents, and your great-great-grandparents wanted you, me, Corey, and Devin to do more than anything?"

"Get an education?"

"Right. And they suffered through racism that we can't even imagine, and even death, just so you could go to school, get an education, and become a productive citizen who adds to society. Not takes away." When her eyes well up with tears, mine do too. "Money is not the most important thing in life, Son. And if that's what you think, then I've failed you as a parent. I've tried to raise you boys in a way that would make God proud and that would make your dad proud—by myself."

She looks down at her hands and takes a deep breath. "Do you know why your dad took a job teaching in Harlem when he could have made more money teaching up here in Westchester?"

"No," I answer, barely above a whisper.

"To reach young black boys who didn't know the value of an education, and to try everything in his power to keep them from dropping out of school."

I feel ashamed and hurt because my dad sacrificed his life to reach people who thought school wasn't important. Then me, his own son, thinks the same thing. If he would've just taken a job up here, he wouldn't have had to go down to Harlem. Then he wouldn't have stayed late to tutor that student. And if he hadn't tutored that student, he could've come home at his regular time. At his regular time it would've still been light outside. Then those guys wouldn't have tried to rob him, and he'd still be here with us.

I grab Moms and hold her. I can't stop saying, "I'm sorry."

5

On Friday the mood in the house for the competition is totally different because me and Moms are the only ones here. Corey and Devin are still at work. I'm not allowed to have any guests, so I'm sure Fat Mike and Cheryl are listening at their house. Boo Boo is probably out in the street.

Moms pan broils tilapia fillets and mixes together her own cocktail sauce. She hooks up another spinach salad with Kalamata olives. No starch tonight, but that's cool. Moms says you have to keep fatty foods, sweets, *and* carbs in check to maintain a healthy diet.

I haven't listened to the radio since Tuesday because my punishment also includes a total media ban (except for the competition). Life without radio is a challenge, but not having TV is worse because this is the time of year when the Knicks' and the Yankees' seasons overlap. Fortunately, it's not football season, because no TV would mean no Giants, and that would pretty much be the end of the world.

49

When Mixmaster Magic comes on the air, the thought of missing an opportunity to make music for his show introduction makes me sick to my stomach. All week the words of the loud preacher have been ringing in my ear. He said your sin will find you out. Last Sunday I was thinking, yeah right. But in this case I guess he was right.

Tonight we're going up against a crew from Virginia Beach called Fly Crime. Then there's a crew from Staten Island called Shadow of Death and an emcee from Manhattan named Scientific. Magic says he's allowing Fly Crime in the competition because they were recommended by Timbaland and managed by Missy Elliot. That doesn't seem fair. With all those connections, they don't need a record deal. But what am I going to do, cry about it?

The winner from the previous week always goes last. That gives me and Fat Mike a huge advantage because the last song people hear usually sticks in their mind the most.

Fly Crime goes first. Their song sounds crisp and clear. You can tell they recorded in a real studio. Conceptually, they're very different too. One rapper, Mr. E, raps about how fly he is, and the other rapper, Treble Fresh, talks about doing crime. They bring that back-and-forth style that Run DMC made famous.

Shadow of Death is straight gangsta. I would describe them as a cross between The Game and Styles P.

Scientific is a pure lyricist. Before his music drops, he kicks a deep spoken-word poem to the sound of dripping water. Once the beat comes in, his rhymes take off and don't stop until the song is over. I don't know how he packs that many syllables into his sentences. His song has no hook, but it doesn't need one because it's that tight.

My big head is in depress mode because of the stiff competition we're facing tonight.

Magic picks a different song for us this week. He chooses "Mount V," which is a song about Mount Vernon. I didn't sample any records on that track. I recorded sounds from a really bad thunderstorm we had last year and mixed it with a recording I made of fourth period lunch at school. Then I played some complicated chords in a sharp key using a synthesized wind chime. The effect is a grimy track that's more like a soundscape. You feel like you're at the edge of the earth staring into an abyss with an anxious crowd watching. Fat Mike's lyrics brighten up the beat because they're witty, and his unorthodox flow sits right in the center of the track. It's the most original-sounding song I've heard in a long time.

When the votes start coming in, it's a dead heat. Everybody's getting votes, and Magic is loving every minute of it.

"Tri-State, it's too close to call, so we don't have a winner. I have to count the votes a second time during the commercial break. Keep it locked right here to Power 97! The Magic is back in sixty seconds!"

A minute is a lifetime when your heart is in your throat. The thought of us losing never crossed my mind.

When Magic comes back on, I feel frustration creeping up the back of my neck. He seems to be squeezing every ounce of suspense out of this moment just to make the listeners squirm.

"And the winner is . . ."

A drum roll goes on for an eternity.

"FAT MIKE!"

I'm dizzy when I let my breath out. I didn't realize that I'd been holding it the whole time. We managed to pull off the vicTory by a single vote that came in during the commercial break.

Moms and I jump up and down like a couple of cheerleaders. As soon as I realize it, I quickly get my cool back in order and take a seat.

That was as stressful as watching my Giants in Super Bowl XLII. Remember the play where Eli Manning miraculously escaped being tackled by the whole New England defensive line and threw the ball to David Tyree for "the catch"? That's the way I was feeling.

Then Magic says, "This next set goes out to my man Terror Tory, who's on lock right now. He's not in Rikers Island, and he's not upstate. He's under house arrest in money-earnin' Mount Vernon. Hold your head, my brother. And Moms, my apologies to you again!"

Moms can't help but smile, and then I break into a cheese grin.

Magic plays "Before I Let Go" by Frankie Beverly and Maze. Then he brings in Mario's "Let Me Love You." After that he cross fades over to Lupe Fiasco's "Superstar."

When I hear the legendary Mixmaster Magic using a mix that I gave him, I feel like I can run through a wall.

On Sunday morning I'm waiting outside of Moms's bedroom door, suited up. She's startled when she comes out because she's not used to anybody being up this early on Sunday.

"You scared the starch out of me!" she says.

"Don't we have to hurry up so we won't be late?"

Moms looks me up and down in my suit. "So you're going to church, huh?"

I can tell by the way she's looking at me that she has me figured out.

"Well, at least you're going," she says, kissing me on the forehead.

When we get to the church, people are still filing in. I scope the place out and try to anticipate where the Lords will sit when they come in. I have to make sure they're not behind me this time. Then I can get a closer look at the girl of my dreams. The last place I want to be is behind her because all I'll see is the back of her head.

I choose a seat along the side of the church where the pews face the main center aisle. I get comfortable and stake everything out, waiting on the Lords. An older man sits next to me.

"You Terri's son, ain't you?"

"Yes, sir."

"Always good to see young men in the church. Congratulations."

"Thanks." I'm not sure what he's congratulating me for, but before I get the thought out of my head, he continues.

"You don't know what I'm congratulating you for, do you?"

"No, sir."

"You doing a real good job in that competition on the radio. My grandson told me all about it. That's him up there." He points out the drummer in the church band. I recognize him as the guy who was doing the human beat box in my ear on Tuesday.

"He goes to my school."

"That's right. And he's taking after his grandfather by playing drums. I was a set drummer for Curtis Mayfield, Roy Ayers, Bootsy Collins. If you can name 'em, I played with 'em." He gives me a deadly serious look. "I'm going to give you a piece of unsolicited advice. Guard your heart. Because out of it spring the issues of life." He pauses to make sure I'm paying attention. "You listening to me?"

"Yes, sir."

"The industry swallows people whole and robs them of they moral fabric. If you were my child, I'd tell you to leave it alone, but you wouldn't listen to me anyway 'cuz you got your heart set on the riches and the fame of it all. I know 'cuz I was just like you. I came up here from Mississippi when I was about your age to make it. And I did. But the mess I made of myself is taking years to undo. And that's why I'm here in this church. Undoing mess. Just remember, son. All that glitters ain't gold."

He steps off as quickly as he came. Instinctively, I write him off as an old man who's had his fun but doesn't want me to have mine. Besides, just because the industry got him all twisted doesn't mean it's going to happen to me.

While I'm thinking, everyone in the church rises to their feet. They all start to sing. I grab a hymnal and flip to the song. I look up every few words to make sure I don't miss my girl coming in. Sure enough, at the start of the second verse, the Lords enter and stand directly across from me in the main center aisle. They immediately join in the singing. My girl knows all the words to the song without even cracking the hymnal. Amazing.

I get light-headed just looking at her. This must be what love feels like. Maybe we can get married and have kids or something. So it's probably a good idea for me to start saving up for the wedding. I hear they're pretty expensive these days. But wait, aren't the girl's parents supposed to pay for the wedding? Or is it the reception? I don't know, but I'll start putting away something for whichever one I have to pay for. I hope she'll be cool with living in Harlem.

Just as I'm about to pick out a venue for our pending nuptials, I get a tap on the shoulder. It's an usher. "Can you let this nice family have your seat and the three beside you? It's four of them and only one of you."

I look over at my girl. She's less than twenty feet away. I want to say no, but my home training kicks in. I reluctantly step into the aisle and follow the usher into the nosebleeds in the balcony.

"Thank you for being so considerate. Enjoy the service," she says before she walks away.

This is not good. I peer over the railing, and the only

part of my wife I can see is the top of her head. I slouch back into my seat and look around. The only thing up here besides me is the audio mixing board.

The loud preacher steps up to the microphone and starts to speak, but no sound comes out of the system. Everyone in the church looks up at me—including my wife. I dash over to the board and quickly survey the channel designations. I see the one labeled "main mike" and bring up the volume.

The preacher calls me out. "That doesn't look like my board operator. That looks like Terri's boy. Where've you been, son?"

Completely caught off guard, I stammer, "Ummm, in school?"

"Well, don't stay gone so long. Come on back. I can give you a job as the board operator since ours seems to have walked off."

The congregation laughs. I look at my wife and she's smiling too, but she quickly looks away when we make eye contact. My heart is set aflutter (I learned how to talk like that from Devin when he was doing Shakespeare).

Back in my seat, I notice that my wife is actually taking notes on what the preacher is saying. I don't think I've ever seen someone my age do that. It seems like she actually *likes* being here.

I watch the top of her head and her writing hand for the rest of the service.

Before we're dismissed by Reverend Frank (I figure I'll stop calling him the loud preacher since he wasn't loud today and he remembers who I am), I head downstairs.

I reach the church lobby just as the Lords are coming out of the sanctuary. Mr. Lord sees me and breaks into a wide grin. He gives me five. I wonder, was turning up the volume on the microphone that big of a deal?

"Tory! You don't remember me, do you?"

"No, sir," I answer.

"I haven't seen you since you were a little baby."

"You know me?"

"Yeah, man. I used to teach with your dad at P.S. 175. This is my wife, Barbara, and my daughter, Precious."

Precious Lord is her name? You've got to be kidding me.

Immediately the words of the hymn start playing in my head. *Precious Lord, take my hand. Lead me on, let me stand* . . .

I have that record too. My dad was from South Carolina, and like most people down there, he grew up in church. Even though he stopped going once he was out on his own, he still had a few gospel records in his collection. And I use them.

I sampled a part of the song "Rough Side of the Mountain" for the song "Mount V" that I did with Fat Mike. The first line in the chorus of "Rough Side of the Mountain" goes, "I'm coming up on the rough side of the mountain." I took "rough side" from the line and built it into the hook, which says, "I'm from the *rough side* of Mount V." And that song is actually true because me and Fat Mike live on the south side of Mount Vernon, right next to the Bronx. It can get pretty crazy over here. It's like night and day compared to the north side. Over there they have really nice neighborhoods with huge houses that cost a lot of money.

Mrs. Lord seems as excited to see me as Mr. Lord is. She says, "You and Precious used to play together when you were babies."

Precious and I look at each other because neither of us remembers. This has to be destiny. My wife and I used to play together as babies, then we're separated, only to be reunited at fifteen to live happily ever after.

Precious and I shake hands. "I don't know if I should say, 'Nice to meet you,' or 'Good to see you again,'" she says.

"We could probably say both," I say.

She reminds me of somebody, but I can't quite put my finger on it. Her smile, her voice, her touch—it all makes me weak in the knees.

The lyrics to the hymn come rushing back to my head like a remixed single. *Precious Lord, take my hand. Lead me on, let me stand* . . . I want her to do all of those.

Mrs. Lord says, "You should stop by the house sometime. I teach Precious at home, so she hasn't made a lot of friends up here yet."

"Where'd you move from?"

"Harlem. We lived in Lenox Terrace, down the street from the school," Mr. Lord says. "We'll have you and your mother over for dinner soon."

I feel like pinching myself to make sure I'm not bugging.

Before the Lords leave, they say, "See you next week."

No doubt, they will.

6

Boo Boo is waiting for me at the gate in front of the school on Monday morning. He has on a brand-new pair of Jordans. I don't remember Boo Boo ever having new sneakers because his foster parents treat him different from their real kids. I've always wondered if they really cared about Boo Boo outside of the check they get from social services each month. His parents are mad strict with their real kids, but Boo Boo can do whatever he wants. He can stay out late and they won't even say anything. That's how he was able to go to Mr. Pisarcik's house and mess up his truck without his folks knowing about it. He can even bring home bad grades and they won't do anything. But when he was younger, he always got really bad beatings for dumb stuff like breaking a dish or spilling something. Personally, I don't think it's right to make differences in your kids. If you can't love the foster ones the same way you love your real ones, you shouldn't take them. If his folks need extra money, they should get a second job.

"Yo, those sneakers are mad hard, when'd you get those?" I ask.

"That's for me to know and you to find out," he says. There's an awkward silence. "Nah, I'm just playing. My moms got them for me."

That's different. Boo Boo always gets his foster brother Lenny's hand-me-downs. But I'm glad for him. Maybe this means his foster parents will start treating him better.

I stick my fist out to give Boo Boo a pound. "That's hot your moms got you some new ones," I tell him, but he leaves me hanging.

"What you trying to say?" he asks, real serious.

"You know, your folks usually give you Lenny's old joints," I say. I'm surprised at his reaction because we've had conversations about this ever since we were younger.

He slaps my hand away. "Somebody else can shine around here besides you." He leaves me standing at the gate to the school.

◆

On Friday Moms decides to have mercy on me and lets me have a few people over for the finals. The whole crew is there again—Fat Mike, Cheryl, Boo Boo, Corey, and Devin.

Boo Boo is back to his old self, and I've decided to just ignore what went down at school the other day. I still don't understand it. Maybe he thought I was trying to play him or something. Boo Boo's had a hard life, and that's the main reason we became friends in the first place. When we were in kindergarten, everybody called him "Boo Boo in the toilet" because some days he would come to school wearing dirty clothes that smelled bad. I felt sorry for him, so I would talk to him when nobody else would.

By the time we got to first grade, Boo Boo was tired of all the jokes. He started beating up anybody who said things he didn't like. After the first few weeks of class, he had taken out everybody in school who was supposed to be hard. There were a few times when he went after people who said things about me he didn't like. Everybody he beat up back then is still scared of him today.

Of course, with all the fighting, Boo Boo got a reputation with the teachers as being a problem. He got his first suspension in the first grade, and it's been pretty much a regular thing since. Now that I think about it, Boo Boo is the first person I ever heard talking about dropping out of school. From what I now know about my dad, Boo Boo would have been exactly the type of student he was looking for.

"The championship menu," as Moms is calling it, is ground turkey burgers and steamed broccoli. Fat Mike is challenged by the food tonight because he's never had ground turkey. And he's not big on vegetables (pun intended), especially steamed ones. He takes one bite of a burger and almost earls on the second one. He says the texture of the meat feels funny in his mouth, and that his mind won't let him enjoy it.

"Do you eat turkey on Thanksgiving?" I ask.

"Of course."

"So what's the difference?"

"Turkey's not supposed to look like burger meat, son. It's supposed to look like—turkey."

Cheryl shakes her head. She goes to private school, so she's more "cultured." If you didn't know her and Fat Mike were sister and brother, you'd never guess they were related. She's skinny, she talks like a valley girl, and she's actually very pretty. Her and Fat Mike do have different dads, though. She and Devin take acting classes together, and I know it's something going on between them. Of course they lie and say it's not. But if you saw the way they're all over each other when they rehearse their scenes, you'd think the same thing I do. Denzel can't even act that good.

I can't front, I'm nervous tonight. After last week, I don't know how much more of this I can take. I'm just glad it'll all be over in less than an hour.

Fat Mike, on the other hand, is parading around the house like he's already a star. He's even wearing sunshades in the house, and it's nighttime. He says he bought them especially for the occasion.

Corey notices and nudges me and Devin. "Moms would never let us get away with that."

"That's my word," Devin says. He looks at Fat Mike and then at Moms, who's busy being the perfect host. "We can't wear hats in the house, we can't wear shoes in the house. We can't even wear coats in the house."

"Coats? Man, we can't even whistle in here," Corey says.

We crack up like a trio of grounded Humptys. Moms has always been a stickler for manners no matter how old-fashioned they are. That's the way it is and the way it's always going to be—unless you're a guest. They must get the manners pass.

It's only two rappers tonight, Fat Mike and Bang Up Black from Harlem. Since it's the championship round, Mixmaster Magic does a coin toss to find out who gets to go last. Fat Mike is heads and Bang Up Black is tails. They mike the whole process so you hear the coin hit the studio floor and roll around until it comes to a stop. It's tails, so we go first.

Magic picks the third song on the demo, "Miss All About Her." That one is about a stuck-up girl that Fat Mike gets by the end of the song. In that beat I sampled a record I found at a yard sale called "Dokhtare Bagh" by the Afghan Ensemble. I laid down an old-school boom bap drum track underneath the sample. Then I brought in some strings. It has a dreamy, otherworldly sound that works well with the concept of this exotic beauty with her nose in the air.

As soon as Bang Up Black comes through the speakers, I know we lost. This dude has a voice that sounds as different as DMX's did when he first came out back in the day. It's deep, intense, and bursting with flavor. And his flow is dumb raw. He links together words and phrases that you'd never guess would rhyme. He does this with a stutter-step style where he divides the syllables of a word over more than one sentence to make it rhyme with another word in the next sentence. It's hard for me to describe. You'd have to hear him yourself to appreciate it.

As a matter of fact, the whole world is going to hear him. He's that good. And I'm not the only one feeling his talent. The living room gets quiet as soon as his song comes on, and nobody moves until it's done.

Magic comes back on the air with a "Wooooooo!" that's as hyped as the one he gave us in the first round. "Tri-State, we should take Bang Up Black's rhymes and put them over Terror Tory's beats! That's guaranteed plati-num!"

Everybody in the room is uncomfortable with Magic saying that, especially me.

Fat Mike has been slumped down in his seat since Bang Up Black came on. I think he knew we lost too. It was obvious. Now Mixmaster Magic is shutting him out of this once-in-a-lifetime opportunity but bigging me up at the same time. One sentence spoken over the air with millions of people listening sends Fat Mike's dreams of getting girls, money, and fame crashing to the ground. He jumps up from his chair, kicks it over, and curses.

Corey and Devin pop up like two jack-in-the-boxes.

"What's wrong with you, breaking furniture and cursing in front of my moms?" Corey shouts.

"Corey, Devin! Sit down!" Moms says.

"Nah, Moms!" Devin says. "He's not going to disrespect you like that!"

Fat Mike is already out the door. Cheryl runs after him. Me and Moms have to restrain Corey and Devin to keep them from going after Fat Mike. And that's the last time I saw him—at least until the drama hit the fan.

You're not going to believe this. I'm riding in the back of a brand-new Chevy Suburban with Precious Lord sitting right next to me. Mrs. Lord called my moms last Wednesday and invited us over for dinner after church. They live in north Mount Vernon, so Mr. Lord must be making cake.

This is my first time riding in a new car, and I don't know what smells better, Precious or the 'burban. She's still getting used to the suburban lifestyle (pun intended) because in Harlem everywhere they needed to go was in walking distance. Mr. Lord had to buy a car when they moved up here three months ago because he drives to work now. He's the new assistant dean of liberal studies and a math professor at Concordia College in Bronxville. That's a long way from teaching fifth grade math at P.S. 175 fifteen years ago with my dad.

Moms is in the second row of the truck, and Mr. and Mrs. Lord are in the two front seats. After every other sentence they bust out laughing. I don't know what they're cracking up about, but it sounds like old times. Me and Precious are in the third row, and I'm feeling like I should strike up a conversation. The only thing we're doing is staring out the window.

I build up every ounce of guts I have only to blurt out the dumbest question in the history of boy-meets-girl. "So, is it boring going to school with your moms?"

Precious turns from her window with a giant smile on her baby-doll face. "I don't go to school *with* my mother, she's just my teacher. And no, it's not boring. My mother is cool. It's like having a private tutor, you know?"

Actually, I don't. They don't have tutors at my school, especially not private ones. I move on to the next question. This time I hope I sound a little more intelligent.

"What about the social part of school, like hanging out and stuff like that?"

"I don't do a whole lot of hanging out," she says. "But the other stuff I do at St. Ursula. I'm on the debate team and the gymnastics team. Next year I'm going to see if I can start a dance club because they don't have a dance team there yet."

St. Ursula is an exclusive private school with a tall iron gate around it. It's where rich people send their kids when they don't want them sitting next to people like me, Boo Boo, and Fat Mike in public school.

"How can you be on a team at St. Urse when you're homeschooled?" I ask.

"New York State law says that homeschooled students can participate in extracurricular activities at any public school because our property taxes pay for the school just like everyone else's."

"St. Urse is private, though."

"It is, but my mother and the principal were roommates in college, so we got the hookup. And they had all the extracurricular activities I was interested in doing except dance."

"So you're like a dancer or something?"

"I'm not a professional or anything. I've just been taking classes since I was three. It's something fun to do, and it'll look good on my college application."

Fifteen and already thinking about her college application. I'm pretty impressed with Precious Lord so far. Maybe now's the time to impress her with a little bit about me.

"So, are you down with hip-hop?"

"Oh, definitely," she says.

"Who do you like?"

"You've probably never heard of the people I listen to."

She obviously doesn't know who I am. Not only am I a self-proclaimed hip-hop historian, I also pride myself on knowing all the hottest emcees, no matter where they're from, even if they're not signed and still on the mix-tape circuit.

She starts dropping names. "I like The Cross Movement, Lecrae, Shai Linne, Todd Bangz, Corey Red & Precise . . ."

She's right, I haven't heard of any of them.

". . . Everyday Process, Flame, J.R., and Da' Truth," she finishes. "There's a few others, but those are my favorites."

"Are they like underground or something?"

She laughs. "Yeah, the catacombs. They're all Christian hip-hop artists."

Christian and hip-hop doesn't even sound right in the same sentence. I picture a dude in a choir robe trying to get his flow on with the rest of the choir singing his hooks. Hip-hop is for the streets, not the church, that's my word.

I'm so wrapped up in our conversation that I don't notice that the streets we're driving on have gotten wider and quieter, and the houses much bigger. We pull into the Lords' circular driveway, and their house is probably six times the size of ours. I see Moms's face. It's not jealousy at all, but the same look she gets when she thinks about my dad not being here anymore.

Inside, their crib is like a museum. It's wood all over the place. The floors are wood, the bottom half of the walls are wood, and they even have wood beams going across the ceiling. Expensive-looking paintings with black people in them are on every wall, and there's African art in each room. The house is popping, no doubt, but it doesn't look like a place where you can stretch out, get comfortable, and eat turkey burgers and steamed broccoli.

"I'm going to take Tory down to the basement and play some music!" Precious calls out. Our folks are laughing and walking into the next room, so I don't think they even hear her.

Their basement is bananas. It's like something you see on HGTV. They have a pool table, a dartboard, a fireplace, and a bar. Precious sees me gawking.

"Pretty cool, right? But there's no alcohol down here because my parents don't drink anymore."

She steps behind the bar and goes to work. She puts ginger ale, cranberry juice, and ice in a stainless steel shaker and shakes it up like a pro. Then she pours it into two oversized martini glasses. She tops off each drink with a colorful paper umbrella, a cherry, and a chunk of pine-apple. As I'm sipping my Precious Daiquiri (her words, not mine), I do a 360 of the room. The other side of the basement looks like a private screening room. There's a plasma TV that covers an entire wall, and seats bolted to the floor like you see in movie theaters.

"This all came with the house," she says. "This base-ment is what made us decide on this house over the other ones we were looking at."

"Is this what your apartment in Harlem was like?"

"No way. We had a really nice place, but it was nothing like this. My parents bought that apartment like fifteen years ago when Harlem was still cheap. Then the value went through the roof. But you get a lot more for your money up here. I'm still getting used to all this myself."

I unconsciously breathe a sigh of relief. The fact that all this Big Willie styling is new to her too makes her seem more on my level. I was starting to get intimidated with the brand-new whip, St. Urse, and this big house.

She hits a button behind the bar, and gospel music floods the room. She frowns. "That's my parents' music. I'm not into that 'old-time religion' stuff." She changes the music, and hip-hop blasts from the speakers. She turns it up louder and starts bobbing her head to the beat.

"This is Everyday Process!" she shouts over the music. "One of the groups I was telling you about!"

I can't front, the song is hot. The beats are banging, and the two dudes rhyming are bringing it for real. If she hadn't told me it was Christian, I wouldn't have known the difference.

"They should play this on Power 97!" I yell.

"What?"

"I said they should play this on—"

She cuts the music off in the middle of my sentence as I scream "Power 97" loud enough to be heard at the station. We crack up into little pieces. It doesn't seem like what happened was that funny, but we laugh harder and harder until both of us have tears in our eyes. Laughter can be like that sometimes. First you start laughing, and then you start laughing at the laughter itself. After that, it's all downhill.

"I'm sorry," she says after catching her breath. "What did you say about Power 97?"

"I said they should play that on Power 97."

"You're kidding, right?"

"No, I'm serious."

"They'd never play this on Power 97."

"How do you know?"

"Because they're talking about God."

"Nah, their label must not be marketing them right."

She shakes her head. "People don't listen to Power 97 to hear about God. They listen to Power 97 to hear about pimping, slinging, flossing, and hoes."

"That's not the only reason. Do you ever listen to it?"

"I used to sneak and listen to it when I was younger

because that's what all my friends listened to. But I don't anymore because what they play doesn't agree with my worldview."

Worldview? What is that? I guess I'll have to ask another dumb question.

"I don't mean to sound stupid, but what is worldview?"

"Basically, what you think is right and wrong. I guess you can say it's how you view the world from a moral standpoint."

"So what does that have to do with the music you listen to on the radio?" I ask.

"If I'm not into drugs, sex, violence, or materialism, then why would I listen to a radio station that promotes that?" she says.

"But how do you figure the station is promoting it?" I'm starting to take what she's saying personally.

"Because 90 percent of the songs they play are talking about that."

"It's not 90 percent."

"Okay, 95. Name me five rap songs that have been on the charts in our lifetime that didn't talk about sex, drugs, violence, or materialism like they were things to be desired."

I recycle all the hits in my head. There's one . . . two . . . three . . . hmmm . . . Okay, I can't think of five right this second, but I can't let her think she shut me up. We just met.

"As long as you're keeping it real, what's wrong with having songs about sex or materialism or whatever you're feeling when you sit down to write?"

71

She rolls her eyes. "Here we go with keeping it real. If I hear that one more time, I'm going to jump out a window. So that's what we've come to—anything goes as long as you're keeping it real?"

Actually, that is a good point. But I can't let her know that.

"Tory, have you even thought about this, or are you just saying anything right now to win an argument?"

Wait a minute, this girl's trying to get in my head, and this is only our first conversation. "Just because I haven't thought about it doesn't mean I can't have an opinion," I say. "And what's the big deal anyway? Most people are just trying to have fun."

To me that settles it, but Precious is relentless.

"Don't you think it's a problem when *most* people are 'just trying to have fun' without thinking about the consequences of what they're doing?"

I don't know why my heart is beating so fast. It's only questions, and she's just a girl . . . Fortunately, I'm saved by the bell when Mrs. Lord calls us upstairs for dinner.

On the way home, the more I think about what Precious said, the more heated I get. I come up with answers for every one of her questions. And I'm kicking myself because I didn't come up with them on the spot. Then I could've shut her up instead of the other way around. Just because she's on the debate team at St. Urse doesn't make what she said right and what I said wrong.

I don't even know if I like her anymore. But one thing I do know is that I'm not going to church next Sunday.

8

It's the last day of school, and I'm in the lunchroom swag splashing with at least ten people buzzing around me, asking questions. The only thing missing is a Page Six reporter and paparazzi. Boo Boo is like my bodyguard, but I think the spotlight always being on me is starting to get to him. At first he was into it because he was getting attention for something other than being able to clobber people. Now everybody is starting to see him as just "Tory's boy."

Even though me and Fat Mike lost the competition, it's still like I won because Mixmaster Magic said that me and Bang Up Black together is guaranteed platinum. Now people want to know if me and Bang Up Black are doing an album together, and what parties I'm deejaying this summer. I take this opportunity to pub the Young Warriors' Friday night block parties. I do make it clear that I won't be doing the first one this Friday, though. Everybody says they're coming through, so it looks like the block party should be the place to be on Friday nights this summer.

Two guys I don't recognize slip in the back door of the lunchroom. That happens because guys from the neighborhood sometimes sneak in during lunch to try and scheme on the high school girls. These two dudes come right up to me, though. One has locks and the other has a baldy.

The guy with the locks talks over everybody else. "So, you supposed to be all that because they shouted you out on Power?"

"Nah, I'm none of that," I respond, not liking the way he's coming at me.

Baldy talks next. "Well, you must think you something 'cuz you standing up here with a crowd around you like you suppose to be nice or something." Baldy is more aggressive, and I'm not going to lie, I'm getting a little nervous.

"You'd think I was wrong if I punched you in the face right now, wouldn't you?" Locks asks.

Boo Boo jumps in. "Wait, wait, wait, I think you getting a little carried away. This man ain't done nothing to you."

Baldy gets back in the mix and turns his attention to Boo Boo. "Was he talking to you, son? We was having a conversation with this man." He points at me.

Boo Boo takes his shirt off, and people immediately start to back away because he has that crazy look in his eye. "That's my man right there," Boo Boo says, "and if you talking to him, you talking to me."

The security guards see Boo Boo without his shirt on

and make their way toward us. Locks throws a punch, but Boo Boo dips and makes him miss. Girls in the lunchroom start screaming. Chairs are knocked over, and backpacks slide across the floor as people scramble to get out of the way.

Baldy swings and catches Boo Boo dead in the eye. In a flash the security guards are there, but they grab Boo Boo first. While the security guards have Boo Boo yoked up, Locks throws a sucker punch that connects with the eye Boo Boo just got hit in.

Boo Boo goes berserk. "Let me go, man! He snuffed me while you was holding me! Let me go!"

The two Mount Vernon cops stationed at our school appear and cuff all three of them. While the cops are dragging them out, Boo Boo is still trying to get at Baldy and Locks.

Baldy looks back at me and yells, "Watch your back, son! Anytime I see you it's gonna be on!"

I don't realize how shaken up I am until security has cleared the lunchroom. My insides are knotted up like a sun-dried afro.

When I enter the principal's office, Boo Boo is still handcuffed and shirtless. Through the window I can see Baldy and Locks getting stuffed into a police car. Boo Boo's eye is swollen completely shut. As soon as he sees me, he goes nuts.

"You a punk, son! Two dudes bank me and you don't do nothing? Get out my face! I ain't trying to see you right now!"

I stand there frozen. Everything happened so fast that I didn't even have a chance to react.

Boo Boo glares at me out of his one good eye. "I said get out my face!"

On the walk home after school, I'm crushed. Boo Boo is right, I should have done something because he was taking up for me.

Even though I saw Baldy and Locks get taken away in a police car, I look over my shoulder to make sure I'm not being followed. When I get to my block, I look around one more time to make sure nobody's tailing me. The block is clear.

Nobody's home yet, so I go in my room and shut the door. I'm trying to figure out who those dudes are and why they have it in for me. I know I've never seen them before because I never forget a face. And they couldn't be just haters who heard me on Power, because they knew exactly what I looked like—they came right up to me. And they have to be from Mount Vernon, because how else would they know what school I went to? Or what period I had lunch?

Now Boo Boo is hot with me *and* thinks I'm a punk. What could I have done differently? By the time I would have jumped in, it would have been over anyway. I could've hit Locks before he had a chance to sucker punch Boo Boo, but how did I know he was going to throw that last punch?

I'm thinking so hard I feel a headache coming on. The knot in my stomach is getting bigger.

Devin flicks on the light. "Why are you sitting here in the dark?"

I look outside and see that the sun has gone down. I completely lost track of time. When I came in the room, it was still light outside.

"Just in here thinking."

"I saw police cars outside the school. What happened up there?"

Do I tell him? What could he do, though? I wouldn't even know who to tell him to go after. Plus, I don't want Devin and Corey to get involved, because if they do it's going to get ugly real quick. They don't play when it comes to their moms or their little brother.

"Just a fight," I tell him. "You know how it is on the last day of school."

Devin looks at me like he's not completely buying it, but he doesn't press the issue. I think I'm going to keep this to myself unless things get beyond what I can control.

After Devin leaves the room, I grab the phone even though I'm not supposed to be using it for another two weeks. I quickly dial, and the whole time it's ringing I'm hoping that Boo Boo picks up. His moms answers.

"Hi, Mrs. Satterwhite, this is Tory."

There's silence on the other end.

"Mrs. Satterwhite?"

"Yes?" She sounds annoyed.

"May I speak to Boo Boo, please?"

"He ain't here. That fool got sent back to Woodfield."

"It wasn't really his fault," I say.

"Fighting on the last day of school when you're on probation is not his fault? He still ain't learned his lesson. And you sound like as big a fool as he is, talking about it ain't his fault. Call back in a month. And that's assuming he'll even be living here when he gets out." She hangs up.

Now I feel worse. Boo Boo's locked up again, and I'm partly to blame. And he might have to find a place to live when he gets out. He's stayed with us for a day or two when he got kicked out before, but our house isn't big enough for him to move in full-time.

◆

Moms always told us that "deception is the skin off of a lie." When I was younger I didn't understand what she meant, but I definitely know now. When you deceive somebody, you don't give them the whole truth. And withholding part of the truth instead of straight-up lying makes it easier for people to convince themselves that they're being honest.

The reason I'm bringing this up is because that's what I did with Moms today. I asked her if I could go up to Woodfield to visit Boo Boo. I told her he got locked up again for fighting, but I didn't tell her the whole story. If I did, she would've started worrying about me getting jumped, and that would've been the end of me doing anything this summer besides staying in the house. But of course she lets me go even though I'm still on punishment because she thinks it's everybody's duty to visit the "sick and shut-in."

The cab driver stops in front of a depressing brick

building surrounded by a cage. The angry-looking razor wire running along the top of the fence bares its steel fangs and glares down at me through the cab window. This must be a mistake.

"Is this the county jail? I wanted Woodfield Cottage."

The driver apparently has no patience for someone my age questioning his inner GPS. "You say Woodfield Cottage, I bring you to Woodfield Cottage. That's $30."

I pay him and get out. This place looks like a prison for hardened criminals. I thought since it was for juveniles and had the name "Woodfield Cottage," it would look like a retreat facility or something. Don't get me wrong, I know juveniles do foul things these days, but sticking them in a place like this doesn't seem like the answer.

I'm seated at the far end of the ratty waiting room, squinting through lighting that would blind a night owl. Boo Boo bops in wearing a baggy prison jumpsuit, ice grilling like he's as hard as a fistful of rocks. As soon as he sees me, he sucks his teeth, turns on the heels of his new Jordans, and squeaks out of the waiting room.

My punishment is finally over, so now my summer vacation can officially begin. I've spent the last two weeks in the house doing chores. I didn't complain too much because it's not like I could go anywhere. And with all my equipment and records locked up and my telephone privileges shut down, I would've just been around here going crazy without something to do.

Moms gave me a to-do list every day before she went to work, and all of it had to be done by the time she got home. I cleaned every room in the house from the baseboards to the crown molding. I mopped and waxed the floors in the kitchen and the bathrooms. I did laundry, ironed drapes, and even spot cleaned the living room furniture. I didn't miss going outside, though, because I'm not trying to run into Baldy and Locks. I can't help but think that if they know where I go to school, they must know where I live too.

Mixmaster Magic is stopping by tonight to talk to my

moms about the things he wants to do with me this summer. He called and set up this meeting the day before my
punishment ended. It's good to finally have something
to look forward to because I'm still wearing guilt like wet
socks in the winter. Boo Boo will be out in about two
weeks, so hopefully by that time we'll be cool again.

I head up to Young Warriors, and Yancy and Carl are
standing outside the rec center when I get out of the cab.
After giving me a pound, Yancy asks, "Why are you taking
a cab and you live only two blocks away?"

"Didn't feel like walking," I say.

Carl gives me a sly grin. "However you get here, we're
just glad to see you, my brother." He gives me a pound
too.

That's a weight off my shoulders. I'm glad they're still
into me being a part of what they're doing. If I wasn't going
to be a big-time music producer, I'd want to be just like
them. I bet if they hadn't started Young Warriors, they'd
own their own business or be working on Wall Street or
something. They're both "put together well," as my moms
says. They can speak the King's English and the language
of the streets, sometimes in the same conversation.

"Mixmaster Magic put you on the fast track to the glam
life when he pumped you up in the finals," Yancy says.
"And when the Magic Man is in your camp, it's only a
matter of time before the sweet smell of success is the
only cologne in your collection."

I try to play it cool on that point. Nevertheless, I feel
the corners of my mouth curling up to my ears.

Carl chimes in, "We need to get more young cats like

you involved with us so we can show the world what the Young Warriors are all about. You heard about Boo Boo?"

"Yeah, his moms told me."

"He's how you found out about us, right?"

"Yeah."

"That's why we put him on the payroll. He's our unofficial director of recruiting, so we can't wait for him to get out. You saw those new Jordans he got?"

"Yeah," I answer, thinking about the conversation me and Boo Boo had about them.

"He told us that we gave him his first paycheck," Yancy says. "And that paycheck is what allowed him to get his first new pair of sneakers. That's a success story because that's what we're about, empowering the youth."

I wonder why Boo Boo lied about how he got the sneakers. That makes him getting mad at me even more confusing. Maybe I'll ask him about it once we're cool again.

I realize that the whole time I've been standing on the block with Yancy and Carl, I haven't thought about Baldy and Locks once.

"So you'll both be around during the block parties, right?"

"No doubt," Carl says. "Essentially, the block parties are community outreach events masquerading as entertainment."

"Our goal is to have at least one interaction with every person in the neighborhood by summer's end," Yancy adds. "That's why your ability to play music that appeals to different generations is perfect for what we're trying to accomplish."

"Just wanted to make sure," I say, as much to myself as to them.

I guess I'll feel safe.

◆

When the cab drops me off at my house, Mixmaster Magic's Escalade is already out front. He gives me a big grin when I come inside.

"Terror Tory. A legend on the rise," he says.

Moms interrupts. "Mr. Wiggins, please don't fill my boy's head with stuff like that. He's already struggling with his hat size without you anointing him a legend at age fifteen."

"Okay, how does this sound? *Uncharted Terror Tory*." He carefully enunciates the last two words, as if to make sure we catch the meaning. Moms and I give him a blank look.

"I want to make *Uncharted Terror Tory* a part of my show every Friday night from 7:01 to 7:15. Tory will do two six-minute mixes that will feature the hot but forgotten street anthems that didn't make the charts in the '70s, '80s, '90s, and today. I'm going to clear out a two-minute commercial block in the middle that we'll sell as sponsorships to the show. Tory's pay will be 3 percent commission on the four commercial spots that run in those two minutes. You figure a thirty-second spot in my show goes for $800, and there are four spots per week. So that comes out to around $400 per month he would get for about fifteen minutes of work per week."

Moms does not look impressed, but I have to fight hard to keep a superhero shout from flying out of my mouth.

"And before you answer," Magic says, "a car service will transport him door-to-door to and from the station."

I'm completely bugging right now because I thought he only wanted me to do new theme music for *Magic Hour*. But now he wants me to have my own show on *Magic Hour*!

"Why Tory, Mr. Wiggins?"

"Two reasons. The first one is the same one I told you the last time I was here. Your son has a gift, and I want to help develop that gift. That's what I do. You ever heard of Pete Rock? He's from right here in Mount Vernon."

Moms shakes her head no.

I try to jog her memory. "Moms, he's the one I was telling you about who used to live up on Hillside. He was part of the group Pete Rock & C.L. Smooth."

"Okay," Moms says. I'm not sure she remembers, but Magic continues anyway.

"Pete Rock was sixteen when Marley Marl put him on his show. At the time, Marley Marl was one of the hottest producers and radio DJs in hip-hop. He passed the torch to Pete Rock, and then he became one of the best producers in the game. Tory has the talent to do the same thing."

"And what's the second reason?" Moms asks.

"Vantage Records is giving me my own imprint, and I want Tory to be my first in-house producer—"

"What's an imprint?"

"An imprint is when you have your own label under

the umbrella of a larger label." He pauses to make sure Moms understands. She nods, so he continues.

"Bang Up Black will be the first artist I'll be putting out, and his off-the-wall style combined with Tory's unique production skills will be something the industry's never heard before. My goal is to introduce a new sound to the hip-hop game. And like the radio show, Tory will have door-to-door car service anytime we have a recording session. All sessions he's involved in would end by 11 p.m."

I can tell Moms is not feeling it. I can also feel myself getting heated at the idea of her messing everything up.

"Mr. Wiggins, I'll have to give this some thought. Can I give you a call in a day or two?"

Magic's big chest moves up and down as he lets out a sigh. He gave a great sales pitch, and it didn't work. "Okay, you have my numbers," he says.

Moms walks him to the door, then comes back and sits next to me on the couch.

"Moms," I jump in before she has a chance to get started, "I know you're not about to say no to everything I've been working for my entire life."

When she touches my cheek, it takes everything in me not to pull away because I know where this conversation is headed.

"Tory, this is about so much more than me saying no. My responsibility as your mother is to train you up in the way you should go, so when you get older you won't turn away from it. That means I have to protect you from things that I think will do you harm, even if you don't agree with it. Does that make sense?"

"No," I say, even though I know exactly what she's talking about.

"So what do you suggest I do?"

"Let me do it. I mean, I'm old enough to take care of myself."

"You're old enough to take care of yourself?"

"Yes."

"Why don't you have your own apartment then?"

"I can't get an apartment at my age."

"So how are you old enough to take care of yourself?"

Her picking me apart like this is only getting me more upset.

"What does that have to do with me doing the show or making beats for Magic's label?" I ask, my voice rising slightly.

"Everything, because another part of me training you is recognizing your talents and providing an environment where they can develop. Who do you think first recognized your interest in music?"

Here we go. Now she's going to corner me with questions that force me to acknowledge something good she did, right in the middle of me being mad at her.

"You did." I sigh.

"And who first introduced you to records and put you in piano lessons?"

"You," I answer grudgingly.

"And I did all of that because I saw that you had a gift

long before anybody else did. We can't forget that the main reason God gives us gifts is to use them to make the world a better place. Making money off of them was never to be their main use."

Are we on the same planet? Maybe she doesn't understand how big of an opportunity this is to use my gifts.

"My music and deejaying does make the world a better place. You should see the people's faces when I'm doing a party. I affect their moods with the songs I play."

"That's exactly the point, Tory," she says. "That's why you have to be very careful what you allow on top of your tracks. Music is so powerful that some people will dance to a nice beat even if the lyrics say rape and kill all the babies in the world. And those lyrics stick in people's heads for the rest of their lives. Foul lyrics are what corrupt minds. The music just allows them to go down easy."

"So if you're saying no, why don't you just come out and say it instead of talking about all this other stuff?" I'm surprised at how angrily that comes out.

"I know you're upset, baby. But one day you'll understand."

I'm so mad right now that a tear sneaks out of the corner of my eye and runs down my cheek. She tries to wipe it away, but I yank my head back so hard that it strikes the wall. I jump up.

"I'm sick of you always trying to control my life! I'm tired of you!"

I bolt from the house and slam the door. I jump off the porch and take off running. I haven't thought about where I'm going. I just run through streets and traffic without stopping. Out of the corner of my eye, I see the front end of an old Bonneville tank dip to the street as the driver slams on the brakes. A half inch more and EMS would've been peeling me off the asphalt like a bubble-gum sticker.

I wind up in Wilson Woods Park by the waterfall and bury my face in my hands. It's dark and nobody's around, so I could just cry and let out everything that's knotted up my stomach for the past two weeks. My sobs would be drowned out by the cars rushing by on the Hutchinson River Parkway, but I don't do it. Crying makes you soft.

After an hour in the darkness I come to my senses. I remember that it's Friday, it's nighttime, and who knows who I'll run into if I make the long walk home. I hop a cab at the edge of the park.

When I get back to the crib, I notice that no lights are on in the front of the house. Once inside I call everybody's name, but no one answers. I check Moms's bedroom and it's empty. Corey and Devin are probably hanging out, but where is Moms? I'm glad I don't have to face her right now, but I'm concerned that she's not here.

I have a tender lump on the back of my head and a headache the size of the Empire State Building. I go to my room and lay down. I don't realize I'm asleep until I hear someone come in the house. After a moment there's a light knock on my door. I expect to see Moms when I open it, but it's Mr. Lord.

"You want to go for a ride?"

"Okay."

"Bring some of your music."

I follow him out and notice the light shining underneath Moms's closed bedroom door.

After we hop in the 'burban, Mr. Lord pops in one of my CDs. He pumps the music up so loud that my beats are screaming at us through the speakers. Mr. Lord bobs his head to the beat. It looks funny seeing this fortysomething, bougie black man getting his bounce on to my tracks.

When we turn onto 3rd Street, everybody we pass stops to check out the knock that's coming down the block. A crew of girls on 4th Avenue break into a dance as we ride by. I smile on the inside because this is hip-hop—creating street theater as you cruise the streets at night, blasting hip-hop in a fly ride. (This is my first time doing it, but I've seen enough videos and heard enough songs to know it's true.)

Mr. Lord turns onto 1st Street and heads into the Bronx. Each time a CD ends, I pop in another one. After the second CD, I can tell that Mr. Lord is not just trying to be down. He's really feeling my beats. We ride for a while before we pull up in front of the abandoned building that used to be the legendary Skate Key. Mr. Lord turns down the music.

"Do you know the significance of this place?"

"Do I? Of course. This was the center of the hip-hop universe back in the day. Every one of hip-hop's founding fathers either performed here or threw parties here."

"I see you know a little something about hip-hop history."

"This is my life, Mr. Lord. This is what I do."

"I used to come here on Friday nights in the early '80s," he says. "You see those buildings over there?" He points out a cluster of projects a few blocks away.

"Yes."

"That's where I grew up."

"You're from the projects?"

"Why do you look so shocked?"

"Because you don't look like the project type. You look upscale. Establishment."

Mr. Lord smiles. "Do you remember Eric B. and Rakim's song 'I Know You Got Soul'?"

"No doubt!"

"Remember the line where he says, 'It ain't where you're from, it's where you're at'?"

"That's one of my favorite lines." I marvel that he actually knows this stuff.

"Me and my friends who made it out of here, that's the approach we took. We were all working to get ahead, or 'grinding,' as you say today. But grinding for us wasn't about breaking the law or getting over on the system. Our parents taught us that it was about having integrity and knowing that if you had solid character, success would follow. But the first thing we knew we had to do was get out of the projects. The projects were where we were *from*, but that wasn't where we were going to stay. That's why it hurts to hear rappers talk about the hood today like it's the place to be. What's your take on that?"

"I don't see anything wrong with repping where you're from. I mean, I'm not going to live in the hood for the rest of my life, but I can't judge somebody else for what they do."

"But you judge people every day."

"Who, me? Nah, I'm not like that."

"Really? Then how do you determine which guys are cool enough to hang out with and which ones aren't? Or which girl you'd give your number to and which one you wouldn't? Don't you have to judge people in order to do that?"

I have to think about that for a minute.

"Okay, maybe you're right," I admit, "but I can't say anybody's wrong for what they do."

"Shouldn't you, though?"

"Nah, I mind my own business. That's what everybody should do."

Mr. Lord gets quiet and looks out his window. I guess I made a good point. He looks back at me.

"Did you know that your dad and I started teaching at P.S. 175 on the same day?"

"No, I didn't know that."

Mr. Lord breaks into a smile as he reminisces. "Out of all the young teachers at the school, your dad was the one everybody knew was going places. He was always the smartest one in the room without even trying to be. As a matter of fact, he bought that house you live in when the rest of us were still renting rooms at the YMCA."

Now I understand why Moms had that look on her face when we pulled up to the Lords' house. Her and Dad started building wealth by buying a house before everybody else did, but after he died, we got stuck in the same place while everybody caught up to us and passed us by. That look was the pain of thinking about what could have been. And my dad had to be on point if someone as cool as Mr. Lord looked up to him. I bet if my dad was still alive, we'd have a bigger house than he does. And Dad would probably be the president of a college instead of just an assistant dean.

Mr. Lord asks me a question and brings me back to reality. "You know why I bring your dad up?"

I shake my head.

"Because when he died, it messed me up. Of all the people who should've died that night, it shouldn't have been him. He's at the school tutoring while the rest of us are already at the bar starting our weekend."

I don't think Mr. Lord is talking only to me. It's like he's reliving what he's saying and talking to himself at the same time.

"He should've just gone home to be with his own kids, but he's at the school trying to help someone else's."

He focuses his attention on me again.

"What happened to your dad was wrong. Period."

I get a little uncomfortable because he's looking at me with such intensity.

"Do you think the two crackheads who tried to rob him thought it was wrong?"

I swallow hard. "No."

"But you and I know it was. And that night, two people got away with murder because whoever saw what happened thought they should just mind their own business."

Mr. Lord's face tightens. A tear runs down my cheek. We both look away.

We don't say anything on the ride back home. When he pulls up in front of my house, I notice that it's almost two in the morning.

"Mr. Lord, what exactly do you mean when you say 'integrity' and 'solid character'?"

"I'll tell you like I used to tell my grade school students. 'That's the dictionary's job, so look it up.' And consider that your first assignment. It's due Sunday after church."

Church? I don't do church. And what assignment is he talking about? "Your mom told me what's going on and what you two discussed. She asked me to talk to you because she thought you needed a man's perspective. Do you want to hear the compromise I offered her?"

"Okay," I answer, not sure what to expect.

"You and I will meet every Sunday after church. That's when you'll turn in your weekly assignment and get the new one for the coming week. If you miss church or an assignment, or if you're late with either, the radio show and the recording sessions go away immediately. Is that clear?"

"Yes, sir."

"And one last thing. I'm in total agreement with everything your mother told you. So what I'm offering is not intended to undercut her position, it's just a different way of achieving the same goal. That being said, you need to apologize to her. Tory, don't ever disrespect your mother like that again. She deserves better than that. She's been through a lot. Your father would turn over in his grave if he knew what you said to her."

I know he's right, and I'm embarrassed that he even knows about it. "Yes, sir."

As I get out of the truck, I turn around and face Mr. Lord. "Thank you for your help. I really appreciate it." I extend my hand and we shake—like men.

When I get in the house, Moms is standing by the door with her arms crossed, but it's not rage she's holding in, it's love and genuine concern. I hug her and we rock back and forth without saying anything for a long time.

"Moms, I'll never disrespect you like that again. And if I do, you won't have to kick me out, I'll leave on my own."

At that moment I realize how much I love my moms. She's the only parent I've got.

11

According to the big dictionary in our living room, *integrity* means "uncompromising adherence to a code of moral, artistic, or other values: avoidance of deception, expedience, and artificiality." Let me translate. *Integrity* means that you don't take shorts when it comes to morals, artistic things, or values. You tell the whole truth, and expedience and being fake is wack in every circumstance.

I look up *moral* and *expedience* because they're the kind of words you've heard used, but you struggle to define them if someone asks you what they mean. *Moral* is "relating to what is right and wrong: capable of being judged as good or evil in terms of principles of right and wrong action." In other words, you can judge whether someone's actions are right or wrong or good or evil based on a set of rules. That's what Mr. Lord was saying yesterday, but what are the rules, and who made them up?

Expedience says "adherence to means and methods that are temporarily opportune or advantageous even when they conflict with what is right or just; specifically self-interest." We call that "going for self," which means that you do you. Whether it's right or wrong or how it affects other people doesn't matter. It seems like everybody's rolling like that these days, and not just people in the hood. But with integrity you avoid going for self like I avoid cheap sneakers.

I look up *character*. It says "reputation, especially when good: of good moral qualities, moral excellence and firmness blended with self-discipline and judgment." There's *moral* and *judgment* again. So character means that your rep is tight. And you do what's right or good because you don't just react. You think about the consequences before you do or say something. That makes it easier to control yourself when you're tempted to do wrong even under peer pressure.

When I put all of this together, it reminds me of something Moms used to yell at us anytime we were acting up: "PATIENCE, MANNERS, and SELF-CONTROL!" I can hear it ringing in my ears now. I guess if you're consistently rolling like that, you'll have integrity and solid character.

So I think I understand what Mr. Lord is saying now. Back in his day the people who made it out of the hood and did big things were the ones who did what was right. And they were rewarded with a good reputation because of their judgment and their actions. They kept it real, but not by doing whatever they felt like doing and justifying it because they were from the hood. They kept it real by not being fake. It sounds like they were concerned about more than just themselves.

But that's not how it is today. A lot of rappers say they talk about crazy stuff in their songs because that's all they know. And having a rep is still important, but in the streets a bad reputation gets you more respect. But how are you supposed to know what's right or wrong anyway? Everybody has their own opinion about that.

This is getting too deep. I'm curious to hear what Mr. Lord has to say about all of it.

Believe it or not, this dictionary stuff is kind of cool. It's like making a beat. You start at one level, but then you have to go deeper to get a full understanding of the artistry or integrity of the track. The different meanings in the definitions are like the different layers of a beat—drum track, bass line, sample, chords—that come together to make one piece of music. So getting understanding is like making music that sounds exactly like the picture that the lyrics paint.

I power up our terminally ill computer and type this as my first assignment.

In church I sit next to Moms because even though my argument with Precious Lord was three weeks ago, I'm still not feeling her. To make matters worse, after service I'm going to have to sit next to her while we ride over to her house so that me and Mr. Lord can meet. This must be what it's like when a marriage goes sour. You can still be cool with your in-laws even though your wife is doing the Cupid Shuffle on your last nerve.

After church me and Precious aren't even in the 'burban good when she turns to me and says, "I want to apologize for not being a very good host. It's rude to argue with your guest on their first visit to your house."

I'm surprised at how sincere she is, but I can't let her know that she had me on the ropes. "It's all good," I say.

She holds up two tiny fists that could barely hurt a fly. "But on any visit after the first one, it's on, so be ready to defend your position." She puts her miniature dukes down and flashes that baby-doll smile.

Okay, I can't front, I still like her. But I do have to come correct the next time we have a domestic spat. It's obvious she got her debating skills from her dad, and since she lives with him she has an unfair advantage. But I'm going to step my game up because I can't let a girl shut me up no matter how fly she is.

After dinner Mr. Lord takes me up to his office. I've never met anybody who had an office in their house. And Mr. Lord's office is nicer than the principal's at my school. He has this important-looking mahogany desk and a big leather chair with mahogany arms to match. He takes a seat to read my paper, and on the wall behind him, I see three degrees in fancy frames. I check out each one. A bachelor's from Howard University, a master's from Brooklyn College, and a doctorate from Columbia University. Between the debating, the dictionary, and sitting in this office surrounded by degrees, it's making me want to have something to hang on my wall.

Mr. Lord looks up from my paragraph. He leans back in his big chair and clasps his fingers together. "Interesting perspective," he says. "You got both definitions correct. And the parallels you draw between artistic integrity, music composition, and getting understanding are impressive. I would have liked to see you do more to compare and contrast the perception of right and wrong in my generation and yours, but other than that it's very good. Do you have any questions?"

Wow, the way he described what I wrote makes me sound like a scholar. I want to learn how to break things down and talk intelligent like that. Mr. Lord does it better than Yancy and Carl put together. I think I'm going to try to sound educated like him.

"Since having character and integrity is about doing what's right and avoiding what's wrong, how can we correctly define right and wrong when everyone has a different opinion about that?"

"Do they?"

"Yeah," I say, but my confidence in my answer starts to evaporate because he's throwing my question back at me as a question. He got me like that Friday night.

"How many people who say that stealing is okay are okay with someone stealing from them?" he asks.

"But what about the people who haven't been taught that stealing is wrong?" I shoot back.

"I don't know of any place in the world where stealing, murder, lying, or cheating isn't considered wrong. And even if you haven't been taught that these things are wrong, you feel wronged when someone does them to you. You can't feel that you've been wronged unless you believe that right exists. To put it simply, you know what's right or wrong because of the inner moral code we all have hardwired in our hearts called a conscience."

My head is spinning because I've never thought about any of this.

"But your heart can deceive you too," Mr. Lord says. "Agree or disagree?"

"I'd have to think about that."

"That's okay. Never answer a question just to give an answer. Always think it through. For next week, I want you to look up *absolute truth*. Tell me what it is and whether or not you think it exists. Type me up one page, double-spaced, then we can discuss it further." He stands and extends his hand to shake. "By the time I'm finished with you, you'll be ready for Harvard."

He can't be serious. I'm just a dude from the hood going to a public high school where half the people who start don't finish. But you know what? Other people's failures don't have to define me. Besides, as Moms says, there's always truth in jest. That means that even if a person says something and they're not completely serious, they never would've made the statement in the first place if they didn't think it was at least partly true.

It's Monday, and I'm staring up the block through my living room window. After what seems like an eternity, a shiny black Lincoln Town Car slides around the corner. When it stops in front of our house and the driver blows the horn, I know this is it. I snatch up my two backpacks and bolt. Before I'm off the porch, the driver is opening my door. This is nothing like a cab. He must be a chauffeur.

He closes the door behind me and slips behind the wheel. After eyeing me through the rearview mirror, he smiles. "Very, very young boy," he says in a thick accent.

"Sixteen in two and a half weeks," I say.

"What part of industry you do?"

"I produce."

I'm not sure if he's curious or trying to play me.

"Vantage Record at your age?"

"That's what's up."

"There's water, juice, and light snack," he offers.

"How much?"

"Free." He laughs. "What station you like me to go to?"

"Aren't you taking me all the way to the recording studio?"

"Not train station, radio station. What radio station you like me to go to during our ride?"

I feel like a bonehead, but I play it off. "Power 97, thanks."

I thought it felt funny with people at school sweating me, but this guy is old enough to be my dad and he's opening doors for me. I'm not used to getting waited on. It actually makes me feel uncomfortable. My home training taught me that I should be opening doors for this guy because of his age.

"Young rap guys have to get used to service because they come from poor background mostly," the driver says. "But once they used to it, they bad, bad news. Demand everything. One guy want me to take him to girlfriend house when label want me to have him to studio at appointment time. When I refuse to take him to girlfriend house, he threaten me. Say his boys find me out and jump me up. But you don't look that way. Too young. Stay humble. It make career last longer."

I must have "advice, please" written on my forehead, because every adult I'm around wants to be Yoda.

I grab a bottle of water and a couple of chocolate thin mints, kick back, and enjoy my first chauffeured ride.

When I get to the recording studio, Bang Up Black is already there writing rhymes on a yellow legal pad with a Sharpie. He doesn't look anything like I thought he would. First of all, he's light skinned, so I don't know what the black in his name is supposed to mean. Second, he's tall and skinny. With a voice as deep as his, I thought he'd be short, stocky, and cut like a deck of cards. He has long, neat, cornrowed braids and a goatee that adds some hood to his pretty-boy looks. This dude has star written all over him.

When he sees me, he stands and gives me the street handshake-hug combo. "Terror Tory? Yo, your beats are so &%$ hard I thought you were going to be some angry-looking &%$ with scars all across your &%$ face."

Man, some of my friends use profanity, but this guy is a human curse word.

"You look mad young," he says. "How old are you?"

"Sixteen in two and a half weeks," I answer, wishing I'd figured out a way to make Moms's eyebrow pencil work.

"It's all good. Age ain't nothing but a number. Listen to this.

> More flows than the Ganges,
> Man, these cats gamble with their raps like craps.
> But my 'come out' roll already sold.
> And the payoff is seven hits when I spit.
> 'Cuz I'm that slinky finesse cat,
> Dog you with my gift of speech.
> Rock mikes for the girls in Harlem, to Queens in
>   Brighton Beach.
> Staten Island and Bronx chicks get in the act too.
> I'm street theater,
> Bang Up Black coming at you."

While he's spitting the verse, I plug my portable hard drive into the studio's computer. I bring up the folder where I stored all of the samples I want to try out for his album. By the time he's finished, I've looped the first four bars of Gary Burton's "Las Vegas Tango."

"Spit that again," I tell him.

I play the continuous sample loop while he kicks the verse a second time. I load a kick drum and snare and tap out a ridiculous drum track. Next I bring in a crisp high hat to ride the rhythm. Bang Up looks at me, and the bottom half of his narrow face disappears behind a king-sized smile. He slaps me five as hard as Fat Mike does, but I'm used to it now. That's the price you pay when your beats are hot.

Bang Up drops into his seat and bobs his head while he bangs out verse after verse, each one catchier than the one before it. I add some spooky chords to the developing track using a mystical synth sound.

Mixmaster Magic comes in, stops, and listens. "Gary Burton, 'Las Vegas Tango.' That's 1971, how'd you know about that?"

"My dad's record collection," I say.

Bang Up gets Magic's attention. "Yo, Maj, peep this verse." He spits his lyrics to the beat, and Magic shakes his head in disbelief. "Y'all aren't wasting any time. I was coming in here to introduce you two, but you're already putting in work."

"Yo, I'm in the zone right now. Can I blaze up in here?" Bang Up asks.

"Let me talk to you for a minute," Magic says.

Magic takes Bang Up into the soundproof vocal booth. I can see from their body language that they're having a pretty heavy conversation. I know Magic doesn't want me to hear what's being said, but I can't resist the temptation to eavesdrop. I hit the talkback button, which allows me to hear everything.

"No smoking in the booth. I can't expose him to that. He's too young." Magic points to a door in the back of the vocal booth. "Your private room is right there. I set it up especially for you so that you can go in there and do whatever. I figured that's a fair compromise. But I have to look out for Tory, he's only fifteen."

Bang Up doesn't look happy with his style being cramped. "I started smoking when I was twelve." He looks at me through the glass and asks me if I smoke. I act like

I can't hear him, and then I front like I'm hitting the talk-back button for the first time.

"You smoke?" he asks me again.

"No."

"You sip?"

"Nah."

He turns to Magic. "So I'm gonna be the only one getting lifted in here? How am I supposed to make a blazing album like that?" (I wonder if he intended that pun.)

I should probably turn off the talkback button now, but my curiosity won't let me.

Bang Up continues, "Blazing by yourself is lonelier than the last female dog I dumped." Of course he doesn't say female dog, he uses the b-word.

I immediately think about the conversation I had with Mr. Lord. Bang Up Black probably thinks it's right to call a woman the b-word, but I guarantee you he'd think it was wrong if you called his mother the same thing.

I've deejayed at least a hundred parties in my life, but all those parties combined didn't have the number of people listening who are about to hear me now.

I'm at Power 97 getting ready to do *Uncharted Terror Tory* for the first time. While I'm setting up in Studio B, I can see Slam Slade in the main studio finishing up his show. This is unbelievable. All your life you dream about doing something and even imagine all the things you'll do when your opportunity comes. Funny how you don't remember any of that stuff when Opportunity is staring you in the face and his father, Time, is smiling as he counts down the minutes until you perform.

I calm myself by putting my records in the order I'm going to play them. I take each one out of the dust jacket and wipe it down with a terry cloth and a dab of alcohol.

Mixmaster Magic comes into the studio. "You nervous?"

I don't even have to answer because my face says it all.

"Don't forget, it's just deejaying. It doesn't matter if you're doing it for five people or five million. It's still the same thing."

He's right. The difference is if I mess up, everybody in the world is going to hear it. This is as big as it gets: Power 97, New York City, across the country in syndication and global on the Internet. Truly, this is hip-hop at its finest.

"Here's how it's going to go down," Magic says. "I'm going to come in with my show introduction, and after I say 'Stand up!' you're on. You'll hear everything I'm doing through your headphones, but keep your eyes on me through the glass, a'ight?"

"Cool."

My moms says that fear is normal, we just can't let it stop us from doing what we need to do. So I suck it up and put on my headphones.

Slam Slade has already signed off and taken us into the last commercial break before *Magic Hour* begins. After the last commercial, Magic launches into his show introduction. As soon as he finishes, I start out with a scribble scratch. Then I let the record go—all the way back to 1975 with Bob James's "Take Me to the Mardi Gras." Hip-hop heads know this song because Run DMC sampled it in "Peter Piper" back in 1986, and then Missy Elliott sampled "Peter Piper" for her smash hit "Work It" in 2002.

I have two copies of every record in my collection, so while "Mardi Gras" is playing on one turntable, I'm back spinning my second copy on the other turntable and starting the song from the beginning. Then I bring in "Peter Piper." After Run DMC's first verse, I go back to "Mardi Gras." When I cross fade into Missy Elliot's "Work It," Magic starts dancing like he's at the 40/40 Club. Nothing gets a DJ more hyped than seeing another DJ going crazy over his record selection, but when it's Mixmaster Magic flipping out, it's beyond brainsick!

Now fully energized and completely at ease, I bring back "Peter Piper" with a transformer scratch and let it play for the old-school heads. Magic is hoping he can get more older people to listen to his show by adding *Uncharted Terror Tory* to the mix (pun intended). I'm going to play the original records that rappers sampled from and then mix in the hip-hop song. Hip-hop heads will be into it because they'll get a hip-hop hisTory lesson through music. Older folks my moms's age will dig it because the original songs that rappers sampled from don't get airplay anymore.

After "Work It," I bring in "Gonna Make You Mine" by Loose Ends, a hot but forgotten anthem from 1986. After the hook, I cross fade into "Take Your Time," Pete Rock's underground banger from 1998. Loose Ends sings the hook on that song too, so the records blend seamlessly.

I know that it's time for the first commercial break when Magic comes in with his signature "Wooooooo!" He motions for me to open my microphone. He didn't tell me I was going to have to say anything.

Magic says, "You're listening to *Uncharted Terror Tory* with

109

the newest member of the Magic family, Terror Tory. Say 'What up?' to the Tri-State!"

"What up, Tri-State, this is Terror Tory. Never taking sides but always taking over—terriTory, that is!" That rolled off my tongue like I'd rehearsed it a thousand times.

Magic keeps it going. "In case you think his voice sounds kind of young, that's because this brother's only fifteen. And not only is he the man behind the mixes in *Uncharted Terror Tory*, he's also the architect of the new sound that will be coming out on my new label, Magic Music. In the next hour we're going to have Bang Up Black in the studio, the first artist who'll be coming out on the label. Stand up, Tri-State, more *Uncharted Terror Tory* is next."

Magic closes his microphone and bolts into the studio. He gives me the street handshake-hug combo. I feel like I'm on top of the world.

◆

There's nothing like stepping into Times Square on a warm summer night. But when you just finished doing a show on Power 97 and the chauffeur's holding open the door to your car, you can't help but feel like you're the man.

As we zoom up the West Side Highway, my eyes are drawn to the George Washington Bridge. It shimmers against the night sky like a diamond necklace on black velvet. Equally as stunning are the lights from the luxury high-rises on the New Jersey shore doing a jig across the Hudson River.

I'm scheduled to be at the block party in less than

twenty minutes. But the only thing I have to do when I get to the rec center is turn everything on. I went by and set up all my equipment before I went down to Power to do my show. I intentionally set up everything facing the entrance gate to the rec center courtyard. That way if Baldy and Locks decide to show up, I'll see them before they see me. I don't really know what I'm going to do if they come, but for now I'll just take a wait-and-see approach.

I told Bang Up Black about the block party, so he's coming through. He's going to perform "Street Theater," the new song we just finished. We want to see how the crowd responds to it before we do the final mix-down. I'm the one who came up with the name and the hook for the song. I sampled his line "I'm street theater, Bang Up Black coming at you," put some deep echo on it, looped it—and voilà, a hit is born.

I've already told Bang Up that this is a community event, so he can't be cursing when he's on the mike. According to him, that won't be a problem because he has experience performing at family-friendly events. I'm trying to imagine Bang Up Black performing for kids and the elderly. I guess stranger things have happened.

When I put the needle on the first record, half of Mount Vernon springs from the cracks in the concrete. I start off with Eminem's new joint produced by Dr. Dre. Before the song is over, the dance floor, which is the entire cement courtyard in front of the center, is packed tight like Samsonite.

It's mostly kids, teenagers, and people in their twenties out here, but there are a good number of parents and older people too. Some bring chairs and coolers, others set up grills. The air is thick with humidity, the smell of burgers, and the excitement of a New York summer night.

My back is to the crowd as I sort through my crates to get the records for my next set. When I turn around, Precious Lord is standing right in front me. Her baby-doll smile brightens my night like a flashlight. This inspires me to spin Parliament's P-Funk classic of the same name. "Flashlight" always gets the crowd jumping. Young and old sing every word.

"Hi," I say, trying to hide my surprise and excitement.

"Hi," she says.

"Come on back."

"Really?" Now she looks as excited as I feel.

I turn one of my empty crates on its side for her to sit on. I fold up the towel around my neck for her to use as a seat cushion. She sits and crosses her legs, keeping perfect posture on a plastic milk crate. Things like that are what have me gone on Precious Lord. I feel proud having a lady like her beside me while I'm rocking the party. I see why rich guys love a trophy wife. They make you feel like a champion.

I do notice that Precious doesn't bounce or even tap her feet to anything I play. She does smile when I do something that makes the crowd go crazy. Despite being bounceless, she's beautiful, and she looks like she's having a good time.

"Is your pops coming through?"

"No, he's going to pick me up when I call him. I told him you were deejaying and that I'd be sticking close to you."

Head, please don't start spinning. I have to be of a sound mind to rock the party.

The words of the hymn flood my brain again. *Precious Lord, take my hand* . . . Before I get to the next line, I'm interrupted by the princess of South Side, Gessie Johnson. She gives me a hug like we go way back.

"Hey, Terror Tory," she says, real seductive-like.

"Hi, Gessie, how are you?"

She keeps looking over at Precious like Precious is moving in on her terriTory (pun intended). When I introduce them, Precious is all manners and Gessie is all cat-eyed.

"Nice to meet you, Gessie," Precious says.

"Same to you," Gessie mumbles. She turns to me and brightens up. "Call me."

She leaves and looks back to make sure I'm seeing how hard she's switching as she walks away. I see it, and there's no denying Gessie is fine, but I turn my attention back to Precious because keeping her attention is more important.

"What did you do to her?" Precious asks.

I shrug my shoulders. "Got on the radio."

I see Bang Up Black as soon as he comes in. And so does every woman in the place. I have to admit, he is cool as ice. He has a few guys with him who strut in, shouting, "Harlem's in the building!" I move quickly to avert a riot.

Brothers in Mount Vernon get wild when cats from out of town come through like they're running things. I bring in our new song "Street Theater" and open my mike.

"Bang Up Black and his crew from Harlem is in the house! For those of you who've been sleeping for the last month, Bang Up Black was the winner of Power 97's Unsigned Hype contest! And this is his latest joint produced by yours truly, Terror Tory!"

Bang Up waves to the cheering crowd as he and his boys make their way to the DJ booth. Quiet as it's kept, I think I just saved a couple of their lives.

Anytime you play a new song when the dance floor is packed, you get the same reaction. There's a split-second, visible pause while the people listen to see if they're going to leave the dance floor or stay. If there's no mass exodus after the first ten seconds, you know you have them.

Five seconds into "Street Theater," the crowd is at full tilt. Bodies are flying high, and heads are bobbing all over the courtyard.

I open my mike again. "Are y'all ready for a live performance of this new joint by Bang Up Black!"

The crowd roars their approval. I switch to the instrumental of "Street Theater," and Bang Up flows right into the second verse without missing a beat. His style and stage presence attracts guys and girls to the front like a magnet—guys for his skills and girls for his sex appeal. His eyes are red and glassy, so it's obvious he's been getting lifted. But it has zero effect on his razor-sharp delivery.

While he's performing, I'm checking out Precious to see

if she's checking him out too. She's listening because his flow is ridiculous, but she doesn't seem overly affected. And I'm glad because even though we're not married yet, I can't have her falling for somebody else before she even realizes that we were made for each other.

Bang! Bang! Bang!

I hear the shots, and without even thinking, I cover Precious like a blanket.

Bang! Bang! Bang!

Bang Up stops rapping and looks around. After two more shots, I can tell that the gunfire is coming from down the block. That doesn't make the people in the crowd any less shook. Yancy and Carl rush to the front, and Yancy grabs the mike.

"I heard that too, people! But it sounded like it was from farther down the block. The Young Warriors are all about community. That's why we're here tonight. We can't let random gunfire chase us into our homes as soon as we start having fun. That's what the thugs want us to do! This summer, Friday nights are going to belong to the community. And we're going to demonstrate that tonight by staying right here!"

I bring in Maxwell's "Ascension (Don't Ever Wonder)," a classic feel-good song. A group of steppers with moves who look like they're straight out of Chicago take over the center of the dance floor. As people gather around to check out their precision steps, the party atmosphere slowly returns (even as sirens are going off in the distance). Score another point for the power of music and a talented DJ with the right song selection.

Yancy and Carl introduce themselves to Bang Up Black. They dialogue for the next several songs and then head inside the center. I never would have guessed that they had enough in common to talk that long.

Bang Up's entourage stays outside and spends the rest of the night hitting on everything that has breath. The guy who was talking loudest when they first came in steps to Precious. He's probably Bang Up's age, which I would say is about twenty, but I still have to let him know that he's out of line.

"My man, I'd appreciate it if you'd leave her alone. She's up here with me."

"Oh, you hitting that, young buck?" he asks, loud enough for Precious to hear. She rolls her eyes and looks away.

"It's not even about that. She just doesn't want to be bothered."

He blows me off. "If you ain't hitting it, you ain't got no say, young buck."

He touches her elbow, and I move his hand away. He gets in my face and gives me a slight head butt. His breath smells like a funky mix of weed, brew, and Juicy Fruit.

"Touch me again, young buck, and I'm knocking you out, for real."

You ever see those cartoons where the character is yoked up from behind and his feet leave the ground? That's what it looks like when Bang Up appears out of nowhere and snatches dude up.

"You crazy or something? That's my man right there!" Bang Up yells at him. He shoves his knuckleheaded friend into the crowd. When he apologizes to me and Precious, he's mad fidgety. He sniffs as he brushes his thumb across the bridge of his nose.

It's obvious that some of the members of Bang Up Black's entourage don't hold their liquor as well as he does. And to think I probably kept the knuckleheaded one from getting jumped when he first came in. And he repays me by trying to step to my wife.

13

On Saturday I'm whipped. I don't get up until after twelve, and I still haven't written the first word on my assignment. I'm not really up to it this week, but I have to complete it if I want to keep my career going.

I break out the big dictionary in the living room again. I look for *absolute truth*, and it's nowhere to be found. When I look up *absolute* and *truth* by themselves and combine the definitions, it doesn't seem related to what me and Mr. Lord were talking about last week. The lazy part of me wants to write that absolute truth couldn't possibly exist because it can't be found in an unabridged dictionary. I could defend my position by saying, "The last I checked, an unabridged dictionary contained every word known to humankind." Of course, if I write that, Mr. Lord will cut me up like a Peppino's pepperoni pie. I'm going to have to go to the library. I've never been to summer school, but this must be what it feels like.

I take a cab to the main library on South First Avenue.

After I pay the driver, I'm suddenly overwhelmed by a flurry of blows to the back of my head. The cabbie speeds off like he's in danger, but I'm the one who's getting hit. I try to stay on my feet, but I lose my bearings as the sidewalk rushes up to meet me.

From the ground I see two sets of feet stomping and kicking me. Strangely, I don't feel anything, including fear. I hear a man's voice yell, "Hey!" and the two guys take off. I see the back of a shiny baldy and a head full of locks running up the avenue. By the time the library security guard helps me up, Baldy and Locks are already around the corner.

I'm more stunned than anything. Corey told me a long time ago that if I ever got jumped and wound up on the ground, to cover my head with my forearms and fists and curl up as tight as I could to protect my ribs. He said that increases the chances I would live to fight again. That's true because my dad would probably be alive if he had done that. I'm not holding that against him or anything, because everything happens so quick that you don't really know what you'll do in a situation like that. Your instincts take over and you just react. My dad was probably taught to fight to the end, even when you're outnumbered.

Me, on the other hand—I probably looked like a pill bug rolling around. But the only good blows Baldy and Locks got in were the hits to the back of my head. Moms always said I was hardheaded, so they would've had to use lead pipes to do any damage back there.

But you know what? If that's the best Baldy and Locks

can do, there's no reason for me to spend my hard-earned money on cab fare. A box cutter is much cheaper.

You probably think I'm fronting, but I feel liberated as I walk into the library. It's like I've passed through some twisted rite of passage: my first time getting jumped. But that's the last time they'll get in free licks on me. The next time they come around, I'll have something for them.

I'm struggling to focus on my assignment once I'm inside the library. The more I think about what just happened, the madder I get. Baldy and Locks are some real chumps. They look like they might be a year or two older than me, and both of them are bigger than me, but neither of them is man enough to go one-on-one. If they're so hard, then why'd they run when the security guard came outside?

I don't think I'm going to be able to finish this assignment before the library closes.

◆

On Sunday I sit beside Precious Lord in church, but she's the farthest thing from my mind. All I'm thinking about is Baldy and Locks and the shiny new box cutter in my pocket. Every few minutes I check to make sure it's there. I know it's not going anywhere, but that doesn't stop me from checking on it anyway.

Mr. Rosario, the owner of the hardware store we've been going to since I was a kid, didn't want to sell it to me at first. He's not stupid. He knows why teenagers buy box cutters. I never answered his question of *why* I was buying it, I just told him why I *wasn't* buying it. (I told him over and over that I wasn't buying it to hurt anybody.) That's still taking the skin off of a lie, because even though I'm buying it for self-defense, if I'm forced to self-defend, I won't hurt just anybody, I'll hurt two bodies.

I didn't have to close the deal, though. After a long deliberation, Mr. Rosario convinced himself that it was okay to sell it to me by saying, "You and your brothers are good kids. I've known you all your life, and you've never been in any kind of trouble."

"Reputation, especially when good"—that's what the definition of *character* said. And I know that the use of my good reputation with Mr. Rosario lacked integrity, but I'm not going to let the fear of getting jumped keep me from doing what I need to do.

◆

After church, when me and Mr. Lord get up to his office, I think he knows that something is going on with me. He doesn't ask any questions, but he does tell me I can talk to him about anything, anytime. I thank him for the offer and hand him my paper. He reads it out loud.

"'Absolute truth is defined as unvarying and permanent truth that applies to all things, all persons, and in every situation, regardless of the parameters or context: a quality of truth that cannot be exceeded; complete truth.'" He looks up. "That's all you have here."

"That's because I wasn't sure what I thought about it. You said never answer a question just to give an answer."

"But what did I ask you to do?" The look of concern Mr. Lord just had when he told me I could talk to him about anything is replaced with dead seriousness.

"You wanted me to look up absolute truth. Tell you what it is and if I think it exists. Then type a one-page, double-spaced paper so we could talk about it."

"Is that what this is?"

I look down to avoid his stare. "No, sir."

"Look at me," he says. "You always look a person in the eye when you're talking to them—no matter how uncomfortable the conversation gets."

I look up at him, and he continues. "It's obvious something's bothering you, Tory. But if what's bothering you isn't going to keep you from going to the studio tomorrow, it shouldn't have kept you from completing this assignment."

What he's saying is right, but I don't like that he's talking to me like he's my dad.

"What did we agree would happen if you were late or missed an assignment?" he asks.

"The radio show and recording sessions would be shut down."

Mr. Lord looks like he's wrestling with a difficult decision. "Is there anything else you want me to know?"

If I tell him what's going on, Moms'll find out, and that'll be the end of everything. But if I don't tell him what's going on, he's going to shut me down, and *that'll* be the end of everything.

I want to drop my head, but I can't. "No, sir."

"Tory, part of being a man is accepting responsibility for your actions, even if it causes you to lose an opportunity. But character is more important than opportunity because with character you'll make the most of every opportunity you get. Without character, you'll blow every opportunity that comes your way."

Mr. Lord stands.

My career is over before it even got started good, I realize.

"So this is the first and the last time you don't complete an assignment I give you, correct?" He extends his hand to shake.

"Yes, sir." I grab his hand and practically shake it off his wrist.

"Same assignment next week, but finish it this time. Excellence, not excuses, son. That's the only way for a man to live."

Today it's hot as blazes, so I go up to Young Warriors to play some ball. Guess who's there? Boo Boo. He didn't even holler at me when he got out. He has a fresh haircut, a pair of new Nike Pelada Lows, a new Enyce T-shirt, and a new pair of Akademiks jean shorts.

"What up, Boo Boo?" I say, extending my hand to give him five.

"A'ight," he answers, leaving me hanging as he shoots the ball.

Dude is acting like he barely knows me. He's obviously still heated over what happened.

All eight of us on the court line up at the foul line. The first two who make a basket pick the teams. Boo Boo drains his shot and keeps his arm extended toward the rim as he steps aside, grinning. He's displaying a confidence that I've never seen. Even though he could beat up everybody, he's never been that outgoing. Maybe it's the new clothes. Yancy and Carl must be paying him well.

The next two guys miss, and I'm next. I launch my shot, and it rolls around the rim three times before dropping in.

"Ohhhhh!" everyone but Boo Boo shouts.

I pick Little Willie (who's over six feet tall), Day-Day, and Ace. Boo Boo gets Todd, Jose, and T Boy. The teams are pretty evenly matched. Around here we run a full. Half-court games are for the weak.

Playing ball in Mount Vernon is serious business. For a town as small as ours, we've had a lot of people make the NBA. I think it's been like seven in the last thirty years. Ray and Gus Williams were the first I remember. (Well, I wasn't born yet, but anybody who's picked up a basketball in Mount Vernon knows the history.) Ray was a starting point guard for the Knicks, and Gus won an NBA championship with the Sonics back in 1979. Scooter and Rodney McCray won an NCAA championship at Louisville in 1980, and both of them went to the NBA. Rodney played with Jordan on the Bulls championship team in '93. Ben Gordon won an NCAA championship at UConn in 2004. He was picked third overall by the Bulls in the 2004 NBA draft, and he's been doing his thing ever since. Every August we have Ben Gordon Day in Hartley Park. I'll be deejaying that event this year.

The game today is mad competitive. Boo Boo's team is scoring more baskets than us, but every time they pull ahead, I drain a three-pointer to keep us in the game. Of course everybody's talking trash.

After Day-Day misses two jump shots in a row, Jose says, "You need to work construction shooting all those bricks!"

A couple of possessions later, Todd takes an extra step as he drives to the basket. Little Willie screams, "You walked like the mailman!"

Ace and T Boy have been going at it the whole game. Their tempers flare when T Boy smacks Ace's shot out of the gym with the score tied at 20.

"Can I get my hand back?" Ace says.

"I didn't foul you! That was all ball!" T Boy says.

"And I'm Lebron James!" Ace snatches the ball away. "Game point, right here."

He inbounds the ball to Day-Day, who quickly forks it over to me. I fake like I'm going inside, and when the defense collapses on me, I do a perfect behind-the-back pass to Little Willie, who's wide-open. Rather than end the game with an easy layup, he elevates to dunk it with authority.

Clank! The ball bounces high off the rim.

Boo Boo grabs the rebound and races to the other end of the court. Little Willie catches him but flies right past him when Boo Boo head fakes and stops on a dime. Boo Boo doesn't see me behind him, so I swipe the ball and dash to the other end of the floor. I go up for the winning layup, but I'm undercut and fouled hard. I crash to the floor, but somehow the ball still goes in. I look up, ready to scream on whoever fouled me like that.

Boo Boo is staring down at me with that crazy look in his eye. "You got something to say?"

125

"Yeah. Game. And losers get off the court."

I'm mad, but I'm not going to fight Boo Boo even though I have my box cutter on me. I can't see myself slicing him up no matter how mad I got. Then I'd be as two-faced as he is. But if he wants to keep acting stupid, then forget it. Since he's been hanging out with Yancy and Carl, got a little job and some new clothes, he thinks he doesn't need me anymore. If it wasn't for me, he wouldn't have even had any friends all these years. But that's cool because I'm not trying to be down with anybody who's not trying to be down with me.

As I walk home favoring my tender ankle, the sun starts to set behind the mangy buildings on 4th Street. Hip-hop, reggae, and meringue spill out of open windows and compete for ear time against multilingual sidewalk chatter and music from cars in the street.

I see somebody up at the park who looks just like Fat Mike. I haven't seen him since he cursed in front of my moms and broke the chair in our house over a month ago. He's leaning on the fence talking to somebody. I can't see who it is because not too many people who have a conversation with Fat Mike are wider than he is.

When I get a little closer, I see exactly who it is. It's Baldy. First Boo Boo is tripping, and now this.

My heart gets hot. Now I understand why Moms crosses her arms, because I feel something ugly about to jump out of my chest. So do I just whip out my box cutter, rush over there, and turn Baldy into zipper face? But what if Fat Mike jumps in because he knows him?

I know how to solve this one. I'm going to get Corey and Devin.

I bust in the front door, and Corey and Devin are in the living room laughing about something. Devin sees me first. "You look like you're ready to kill somebody. What's wrong with you?"

Corey, the craziest one out of all of us, stands up. He looks mad, and I haven't even said anything yet.

"This dude that jumped me is up at 4th Street Park with Fat Mike."

"Jumped you?" Corey comes over and starts examining me, starting with my face. I pull away.

"It happened Saturday when I was at the library."

"Don't say anything else," Devin says.

Moms comes in the house with her arms full of groceries as we're heading out the door. Her surveillance skills kick into high gear. "Corey, Devin, Tory, where are you going?"

"We'll be right back, Moms," Corey says, completely emotionless.

Moms gives us an icy eye of the storm. "I didn't ask you how long, I said *where*?"

"We'll be right back," Devin says, as flatly as Corey did. The two of them take off up the block.

I look at Moms before I run after them. She screams for us to come back. Her shouts become more frantic and fainter the farther away we get. In a flash it dawns on me that this is Moms's greatest fear: losing her three sons the same way she lost her husband—in the street.

I stop and turn around. We're far enough away that I

can't hear her anymore, but her body language is scream-ing for us to come back.

"Tory, come on!" Corey's angry demand mixed with the rage that's still in my chest drives me to run to the park even faster. By now the sun has been completely rubbed out by a New York night.

Fat Mike and Baldy are still at the park rapping back and forth to each other. It's like they're onstage, trapped in the spotlight of a streetlight, drowning in its funky orange glow. Just as we roll up, they finish and give each other a pound. Fat Mike's back is to us, so Baldy is the first one to see us emerge from the darkness. His face goes from grin to grim. That's when Fat Mike turns around. He tries to make nice because he knows that Corey and Devin were two seconds off of him when he disrespected our house and our moms in the process.

"What up, Tysons?" Fat Mike asks, as if we're one big happy crew.

"You and your punk friend jumped me!" I growl to Baldy, stepping to him with my hand in my pocket. My sweaty, trembling fingers are choking the life out of my virgin box cutter.

Devin pulls me back and asks Baldy, "Where's your punk friend?"

"I don't know," Baldy says with a defiance that I can see right through. The fear I saw in his eyes when we first rolled up is what was true. He's trying to keep his rep intact since he's going to get smashed anyway.

"Since you don't know where your friend is, you're going

to get it twice," Devin says before turning to Fat Mike. "And you had yours coming for a while now."

"Hold on," Corey breaks in. "Before we start swinging, I want to know what happened."

Is this calm that Corey's displaying just a prelude to a violent explosion?

Fat Mike starts spilling the beans like a cheap paper plate. "I didn't tell them to do nothing," he says. "They came up with this whole thing on they own."

"Came up with what on their own?" Corey asks, looking annoyed.

"Tavaris and Trap was mad when I lost 'cuz I was going to put them on after I got signed. So I was mad and they was mad. But they wanted to take it out on Tory 'cuz Magic put him on instead of us. Jumping him was their idea, not mine."

"Did you know they were going to do it?" Devin asks.

"Well . . . I mean . . ."

I'm furious, so I jump back in. "You told them what school I went to and what lunch I had, didn't you!"

Fat Mike doesn't say anything because he knows he's caught. Baldy dashes toward the park exit, and Corey runs after him. Fat Mike runs in the other direction with Devin on his tail.

It's no way Corey is going to catch Baldy, he's too fast. Baldy gets to the exit just as two Mount Vernon police cars screech to a halt. I drop my shiny new box cutter in the trash can.

Four cops jump out with guns drawn. "Get on the ground!"

The first one trains his weapon on Baldy, who dives to the ground. A second cop points his gun at Corey. My blood runs cold.

"Put your hands on your head and get on the ground!" the cop shouts at my brother, the math whiz, the one with the full scholarship to the same college my dad went to. Corey stops but doesn't get on the ground. He's just standing there looking confused in the blinding light of the police cars.

The cop shouts again, "You got two seconds to put your hands on your head and get on the ground!" His trigger finger is locked solid.

Just then Moms runs up, and the third cop grabs her. I don't think, I just react.

"Get off my moms! Take your hands off my moms!" I shout as I run toward the chaos. The fourth cop has his gun pointed at me now, but all I see is a man getting rough with my mother. Everything is in slow motion.

Moms is hysterical. "Corey, Tory, get down!" She screams at the officer who's holding her, "I'm the one who called you! Please don't shoot! Those are my babies, don't shoot them!"

The blast of a gun brings everything back into real time. Corey and I both fall to the ground. The fourth cop lowers his gun.

I'm facedown on the concrete getting handcuffed when it dawns on me why so many of us get shot by the cops. Two different cultures clash, things escalate and then spin out of control like a record flying off a turntable.

Me and Corey are taken to the station, given a mug

shot, fingerprinted, and put in a holding cell, then the police hear our story and let us go. But I have to admit that it's impossible for any cop to show up at a scene that chaotic and know the complete story. The scariest part is that me or Corey could have been dead before the whole truth had a chance to come out. Cops are trained to fire their weapons only when they think lethal force is necessary. So something—or someone—made that officer fire into the air and see Corey and me as people no different from him, with lives, a family, and a future that we deserve to live.

In the cab on the way home, Corey concentrates on what's passing by his window and I focus on what's happening outside of mine. When we pull up to the house, Moms and Devin are on the porch waiting for us.

Corey takes a deep breath, looks at me, and forces an uncomfortable smile. "Crazy night, right?"

I don't say anything because we both know that's just nerves talking.

"I guess we better go inside," he says.

Moms and Devin meet us at the bottom of the steps, and we all embrace without a word. Once we're safely inside, Corey takes Moms's hand. He can barely look her in the eye. His lips start to quiver, and his voice cracks.

"Moms . . . I'm so sorry . . . putting you through something like that . . . ."

She quiets him with a firm whisper. "It's okay, baby. The only thing that matters is that you and Tory are *here*."

That one word makes my surreal recollection of everything that went down terrifyingly real. Corey breaks and tears come. Moms pulls him close.

"Get it all out, baby. Go ahead and let it all out."

My nose starts burning, so I take a deep breath to try to swallow back my emotions. I'm not successful, and neither is Devin. Two perfectly round balls of water roll down his cheeks. We make eye contact and look away, too embarrassed to see the other cry.

Strangely, Moms is the only one with dry eyes. Her face is masked with an iron toughness.

At that moment I realize that she's stronger than us. And her strength comes from learning how to live with the painful scars that tragedy leaves behind.

The four of us grab each other again, gripped tightly by the realization of just how much we love one another. This hug releases all of the restless butterflies trapped in my stomach.

For the rest of the night, nothing is said. The magnitude of what *could've* happened keeps us silent.

◆

The first thing in the morning, I'm back at the park. I have to get that box cutter before a homeless person or a scared teen like me finds it. The last thing I want is for something I bought to be used to hurt anybody.

I dig through beer bottles, take-out containers, tobacco from blunt cigars, and moist stuff—I don't even want to think about what that is. I'm holding my breath, arm deep in earl-inducing squishiness, when I feel it. I remove the filthy box cutter and toss it in the sewer.

I don't know why I'm thinking this, but maybe Moms

is on to something with this guy-in-the-sky stuff. I still don't understand why he let my dad get killed, but I got jumped from behind by two guys just like he did and didn't get a scratch on me. Could the guy in the sky be the someone who kept that cop from shooting me and Corey last night? If so, I don't need a box cutter. But that's not me anyway, because desperation can make you do crazy things.

And I don't have to worry about Tavaris and Trap anymore. They're going to be spending some time up at Woodfield. It ends up I wasn't the first person they'd assaulted.

14

I open my eyes and slide a mirror from underneath my pillow. I check above my lip for new growth and examine my Adam's apple to see if it's gotten any bigger. As far as I can tell, there's no sign of a mustache, and when I say, "Mike, check one, two, one, two," it doesn't sound like my voice is any deeper.

This is my annual ritual. The night before my birthday, I put a small mirror under my pillow to take out as soon as I wake up. This allows me to see if I've matured physically. To see if I've matured in other ways, I think back on whether or not I reached the goals I set and ask myself, "Do you know more than you did this time last year?"

Here are the goals I had for my fifteenth year. I wanted to finish tenth grade still on the honor roll, because even though I planned on this being my last year, I wanted to create a paper trail that showed I didn't drop out because I was stupid. I accomplished that—my average on my final report card was a 90. Moms wasn't happy because she says I'm smart enough to have at least a 98 if I would just apply myself. She's right, but the last time I checked the alphabet, a "B" was still a "B."

My second goal was to have my music played on some radio station at least once. It didn't matter what station, it could've been ham radio for all I cared. I quadruple accomplished that. I never would've guessed in a million years that my beats would get played on Power 97.

My third goal was to deejay at least five parties for new clients who I didn't know on my last birthday. I blew that one out of the water too because I do *Uncharted Terror Tory* and the Young Warriors parties every Friday night. Technically, the radio show isn't a party, but I didn't know Yancy, Carl, or Mixmaster Magic a year ago.

I definitely know more than I did last year. I can comfortably define *character* and *integrity*, I see how different the hood is now from the way it used to be, and I know how to record in a professional recording studio. I also know how to do a show on the number one radio station in the country. But the most important thing I know now is who my wife is. Even though *she* doesn't know it, I still do.

Moms knocks on my door and interrupts my process. "Tory, telephone."

On my way to the phone, I stop in front of the mirror to flex. No new muscles, but I still look okay.

"Happy birthday," Moms says. She manages to sneak in a kiss before she hands me the phone. I make sure I groan loud enough for her to hear *before* I tell her "thank you." (And I only thank her because my home training demands it.)

Me and Moms go through this every year. She knows that to me, my birthday is no different from any other day. The birthday greetings and all the unnecessary attention embarrass me. That's why I don't tell anybody when my birthday is. I'm amazed at people who actually tell you it's their birthday just so you can say something to them, give them something, or treat them differently for a day. That sounds like an emotionally needy person to me, but to each his own.

I answer the phone, still annoyed at Moms's annual insistence on acknowledging the day I showed up in her life.

"Hi, Tory, it's Precious Lord. I got your number from my mother."

I'm so surprised and excited that I break into song. "Precious Lord, take my hand. Lead me on, let me stand . . ." That's all I get out before she groans as loudly as I did with Moms.

"*Please*, don't do that," she says. "I've been hearing that *my entire life*!"

I've been dying to do this since the day we met, so I continue, "Through the storm, through the night, lead me on to the light. Take my hand, precious Lord, lead me home."

I hear a dial tone, and I'm not sure how long ago she hung up. I hit caller ID and call her right back.

"Hello?" She does not sound amused.

"Precious, I'm sorry." There's still a whiff of a snicker in my voice even though I'm trying hard to keep it weighty.

"It's not funny, Tory. You don't know what it's like when people sing that song every time they find out your name."

"Really, I am sorry. I just couldn't help myself."

There's a moment of silence, then Precious starts singing.

"Happy birthday to you! Happy birthday to you! Happy birthday, dear Torrrrrrrryyyyyyyyyyyyy!"

It's obvious she's trying to get me back, so I let her have her fun.

"Happy birthday to you!" She busts out laughing.

"Touché. We're even now. You must've heard me and my moms on the phone."

"I didn't know today was your birthday."

"Nobody knows, that's intentional."

"I was calling to see if you were up to going somewhere today, but I don't want to intrude on your birthday plans. I'll just see you on Sunday."

"No, no, no. I never make plans on my birthday!"

I hope that didn't sound too desperate. I can't lose any cool points now, not with a potential date on the line (pun intended).

"You want to go to Rapfest?" she asks. "I know it's last minute, but I go every year, and I remembered that you were into hip-hop too."

"What's Rapfest?"

"It's an all-day Christian hip-hop event in the Bronx. You'd like it, you should come."

I do like hanging out with her, but I'm not trying to be trapped in church all day and then turn around and be back again tomorrow. That's the kind of stuff my moms does.

"All day, huh?"

"Yeah, but it's outside. There'll be food, performances, vendors. It's like a cross between a concert, a street fair, and a cookout."

It's outside, so that makes it a little better. I guess I have to suck it up and just go. I'm sure there are going to be times when we're married when I'm trapped in a mall for hours while she's shopping, or cooped up in someone's crib for bridal and baby showers. I might as well learn how to grin and bear it now—and do it convincingly—rather than wait until I'm in my twenties.

"Alright, I'm down. Where do you want to meet?"

"My dad is going to give us a ride down there. I told him we could catch the train back."

Is that excitement I hear in her voice? I wonder if that's because she likes me or because I agreed to go to this church thing. Christians are masters of the bait and switch. They invite you to something like they're really interested in being around you, but what they really want to do is turn you over to Jesus.

"We'll be by to pick you up at noon, is that okay?"

I check the clock. That gives me two hours to get ready for our first date.

"Cool, I'll see you then."

The egg crates are already off the wall, so I jump right in the shower. Once I'm out I can't figure out what to wear. It's church, but she says it's not. I could call her back and ask her what she's wearing, but I don't want her to think

I'm some metrosexual who's going to fight her for mirror space once we're married. I'm just going to be me. I put on a white Ralph Lauren Wings rugby shirt, a pair of Girbaud jean shorts, and a crisp pair of snow-white Reebok classics with ankle socks.

I'm on the porch waiting at 11:59. Mr. Lord and Precious pull up, and she looks like a roll of dimes, plus a few dollars more. She usually lets her coffee-brown hair hang down around her shoulders, but today it's pulled back into a ponytail. This highlights her face, which looks like the pear-shaped diamond on Moms's wedding ring. She blushes when she sees me, and I can't front, I blush right back. Her cocoa complexion is airbrush perfection in the blazing Fourth of July sun.

When I climb into the 'burban, I notice that we're practically dressed alike. We must be soul mates, or is it kindred spirits? Whichever one it is, that's what we are. Precious is rocking a white Ralph Lauren tennis polo, Lauren midcalf jeans, and white Reebok Mule walkers. I won't ever need to do a casting call for any music video I do. I'll just put in a call to Precious Lord, and it's a wrap.

Mr. Lord asks me if I brought any of my music.

"No, sir," I say.

"You're going to a hip-hop event and didn't bring any of your music?"

I don't want to bust his bubble, but I'm rolling with Power 97 and Bang Up Black. I'm not trying to be politicking with no church rappers. No disrespect, but I still don't understand the connection between rap and church.

That's like gangsta square dancing or a hip-hop bar mitzvah.

We pull up beside a car at the light. Precious rolls down her window, and the driver is blasting "Street Theater."

"Tory, isn't that your song?" she asks.

"Mr. Lord, could you turn on Power 97?" I ask.

He turns to the station, and there it is—my beat and Bang Up Black's lyrics. This will go down in hisTory as the best day of my life: rolling in a fly whip with my wife and father-in-law, and seeing someone in their car blasting my song while they're listening to Power 97.

I'm smiling so hard my cheeks start to hurt.

"Mr. Lord, can I use your phone?"

I dial Magic and he picks up. "Hey, it's Tory. I'm listening to 'Street Theater' on the station. How's that possible?"

Magic giggles like a fat man at a free buffet. "I'm pollying hard, little man. I got the song in rotation on everybody's show. I'm running it as a 'coming soon from Magic Music' promo. I just started that yesterday, and it's already the third most requested song on the air! Stay tuned, little man. I'm out for the Grammy on this one. I gotta run. Holler at me later."

I flip the phone shut. What a way to start the age of sixteen.

When we get a block away from the church, Precious goes into adult teenager mode. "Okay, Daddy, we can walk from here."

"I can take you all the way."

"I know, but I'd rather walk in than have my dad drop me off."

"So I'm good enough for the ride down, but when you get close to your destination, you treat me like a pus-filled blister?"

"That is overly dramatic and extremely gross, Daddy. Can't we just walk from here? You were a teenager once. You know how it is."

He does.

Precious gets out first. Mr. Lord taps me on the shoulder as I climb out of the backseat. "She told me how you protected her at the block party. I appreciate that. I can trust you to get her back home safely?"

"Most definitely."

The sidewalk is vibrating when my feet hit the street. I hear a reggaeton beat and we're still a full block away. Precious starts bouncing to the rhythm.

"That's Christian?" I ask.

She doesn't answer, she just nods because she's wrapped up in the beat like a Barbie in a Chanel bomber. She's actually nice with the dance moves too. I'm impressed. It's my first time seeing her get her groove on because she never danced at either of the block parties where I saw her.

There are tons of people walking in the same direction we're going. They're rocking do-rags, braids, Tims, and all the latest hip-hop styles.

"These people don't look like church folks, they look like they're from the streets," I say.

"Of course they're from the streets," Precious says. "Where do you think we are, the Poconos?"

Okay, my statement was dumb. Anywhere you live in

New York City is the streets. You step out of your house and you're literally *on the street*. I guess I'm just surprised to see Christians who don't look corny.

There's a dude walking straight toward us who couldn't possibly be a Christian, though. He looks like a straight-up killer. He has a scar on his face that goes from the corner of his right eye all the way down to his neck. He's built like a Mack truck and tatted up too. I'm trying to figure out what I'm going to do if this crazy-looking dude doesn't step out of our path.

Precious spots him. She screams and runs toward him. He smiles and his ice grill melts when Precious jumps into his arms.

She's playing me. I guess what they say about nice girls is true—they like bad boys. That's probably why she wanted Mr. Lord to drop her at the corner.

I feel like a sucker standing here while Precious and this guy play catch-up. I'm kind of heated too. I came all the way down here to an event that I didn't even want to go to, only to witness the girl I *thought* I wanted to marry in the arms of another man.

Finally she remembers I'm standing here. "I'm sorry, Tory. This is my cousin Baron. I haven't seen him in a loooong time. Baron, this is my friend Tory. His dad and my dad used to teach together at P.S. 175."

Baron shakes my hand with a bone-breaking grip. "What up, little man? Nice to meet you."

"Nice to meet you too," I say, relieved that I wasn't just a party to a secret rendezvous.

"I go on in a few minutes, so I'm going to have to catch

up with y'all later." He kisses Precious on the cheek and gives me a departing handshake that makes all twenty-seven bones in my hand sing for mercy in falsetto. He turns around and bops in the direction of the music.

"He's a Christian?" I ask, massaging my throbbing hand.

"He is now. You know how there's always a black sheep in the family? Well, Baron was ours. The rest of my family is all bougie, but Baron was the one rotten egg. He used to—" She stops. "He's been saved for a few years now, but I don't want to put his dirt in the street."

This day is getting crazier by the minute.

All three blocks in front of the church have been closed off. It's literally thousands of people out here. There's a concert stage in the middle of the center block with stage lighting, video monitors, and everything. The reggaeton beat has been replaced by a hip-hop track. There's this DJ onstage called the Blessed Kept Secret cutting it up on the 1s and 2s. A hype man throws giveaways into the crowd.

It takes a lot to surprise me, but this scene completely blows me away. If I didn't know any better, I'd think I was at a smaller version of Power 97's Summer Fest. These people really seem to be into hip-hop.

I'm still looking around staring at everything when Precious grabs me and pulls me through the crowd. "Baron's onstage," she says.

After a minute of meandering through this maze of Christian hip-hop heads, we get a spot near the front. The Blessed Kept Secret is now back spinning a break beat from Bob James's "Nautilus." I have to admit, he's got skills.

Baron grabs the mike. "What up, Rapfest?"

The crowd roars. The same electricity I feel at any other rap show is here, but it's something else going on that I can't put my finger on.

Baron continues, "For those who don't know, my name is X Wretch. I used to tote big gats and rob rough cats, but after God changed me, I changed my name. X Wretch is from the line in the song 'Amazing Grace'—how sweet the sound that saved a wretch like me."

More cheering. This dude has the crowd in the palm of his hand.

"But I don't want y'all to get it twisted. We're not out here trying to prove that our hip-hop is better than the hip-hop that doesn't include Christ. But we are here to prove that the truth that's in our hip-hop blows their truth out of the water. And that's the truth of the eternal throne holder, Jesus Cristo."

All three blocks erupt into a deafening roar. Even though Baron is talking about Jesus being the truth, it's almost intriguing. I've never seen anybody who looks as thugged out as him talk about religion, especially not in my language.

"So I figure that since rap is one of the most powerful forms of communication, why not use it to communicate the highest truth known to man?"

The beat drops, and Precious goes crazy, clapping and jumping up and down with the rest of the crowd. It's so hyped out here that I'm tempted to jump too, but you know I'm too cool to be jumping for Jesus.

But real talk, Baron has the command, the look, and the stage presence of a 50 or a Tupac. And when he starts spitting, he's on some different stuff I've never heard before.

> God is haunting you with his intangible reality.
> The terrifying reality is God.
> 145th and St. Nick in Harlem,
> Unsaved cats acting hard. You wanna know hard?
> God stretches sky over empty space and hangs
>   the earth on nothing.
> He wraps clouds around the face of the moon.
> He writes eternity with an iron pen in the rock of
>   forever.
> The soon-coming king is coming soon.

His lyrics have me shook. He's making the guy in the sky seem . . . bigger than reality—almost scary. Like a colossal terror moving in on my puny little universe. I'm tripping. It's just lyrics, but X Wretch keeps them coming.

> Eternity stares you in the face when you close
>   your eyes for the last time.
> You'll give an account for every single one of
>   them lies in your last rhyme,
> And you're mistaken if you think that this is only a
>   rap show.
> When you're dead—it's too late to see it's minis-
>   try, yo.

>   If you died right this second, the next, where
>   would you go?

I start thinking about getting jumped the same way my dad did. Then I think about that cop pointing the gun at me and Corey. What if I would've died that night? Where would I be right now? And where is my dad right now?

I know this is going to sound crazy, but I drop my head and get a little misty. Maybe I do believe in life after death, but is heaven and hell real or just some fairy tale?

Before I can try to hide my damp eyes, I feel different people's hands on my shoulders. I don't know what that's about, but I can't let my emotions get the best of me in a crowd full of strangers. And I definitely don't want Precious to see me.

I wipe away the tears and check to see if Precious caught me choking up. She looks dead at me and then tears up too. She grabs my hand, but not in a romantic way. It's like support or something.

But I have to snap out of this. I can't be crying like a punk in front of the girl I'm trying to impress. I take my hand back.

The whole train ride to 241st Street, I don't say anything. Fortunately, Precious doesn't say anything either. I'm still a little weirded out by what happened. People breaking down at church is the kind of stuff you see on those Christian TV channels. Technically, it wasn't church, but still . . .

When we get off the train, the two of us take a cab to Precious's house.

"Thanks for coming," she says.

"Thanks for inviting me," I say, too embarrassed to even look at her.

"So I'll see you tomorrow at church?"

"I don't have much of a choice."

She gets out of the cab. I tell the cabbie not to pull off until she's safely inside. Precious waves and disappears into the house.

Precious hasn't come to any more Young Warriors block parties since the gunshots and drunk knucklehead fiasco. That's probably a good thing because the more of these we do, the less they're like community events. Each week there's fewer kids, older people, and parents, and more hoochies, hustlers, and party animals.

That's because my popularity from *Uncharted Terror Tory* has grown, and "Street Theater" is blowing up all over the airwaves, so word of the block parties has spread. And it's not just a Mount Vernon thing anymore. People are coming from all over the Tri-State to hear me spin. Fortunately, there haven't been any problems even though the crowds are getting bigger and rowdier.

Every night I have at least fifteen people around my turntables. They go buck anytime I do some turntablism or play a mix they heard me do on my show. But you know the craziest part of all of this? The girls. I've never gotten this much attention before.

Tonight there's a young lady staring at me like she wants to have me for dinner. Judging from how she's dressed and the way she's built, she has to be at least twenty-one. When I put on Keyshia Cole's "Playa Cardz Right," she sashays over to me with a catwalk strut, each of her steps perfectly timed to the beat.

"Terror Tory, you've been rocking my world *all night*."

"Thanks, that's what I'm here for."

"Well, I'd like to return the favor."

The girls I know are nowhere near this forward, so I'm caught off guard. I think she mistakes my look of surprise for not understanding what she's offering.

"What I'm saying is that I'd like to do to you what you've been doing to me."

I try not to blush, but I can't help myself. What guy doesn't like an attractive woman in a baby-doll T, low-cut jeans, and a navel ring flirting with him?

"Where are you from?" I ask, trying not to expose the fact that I'm a romance rookie.

"Hempstead. I drove all the way out here with my girlfriend to hear you do your thing."

Just then her girlfriend walks up, and she's fine too.

"Shavonne, you know that boy is only sixteen. Are you trying to go to jail?"

Shavonne pinches my cheek. "He's just so cute. I'd like to teach him a few things."

Her friend grabs her by the hand and practically drags her away. Shavonne looks back and blows me a kiss.

I'm feeling cocky, so I return the favor.

This happens at least once every Friday night. Believe

me, it's mad tempting and a huge ego boost, but I can't cheat on my wife.

I can't lie, though—a part of me wishes this would've happened before I met Precious Lord. And what's wild is that Moms always tried to convince me, Corey, and Devin that you should always be faithful to your husband or wife (including before you meet them) until death do you part. I wasn't planning on doing that, *and* it sounded crazy—until Precious came around. I might be sold now, though, because even though we aren't together, if she got with somebody else right now, I'd be hurt. And straight up, I'd feel like she was wrong. Just like I'd be wrong if I got with one of these girls who's sweating me. Call me crazy, but I'm just keeping it real with y'all.

But back to the party. It's so crowded tonight that Yancy and Carl are concerned that the police are going to come and shut us down. Whenever there's any mention of the police, Yancy and Carl go loco. They say that police in communities like ours always cause problems because they don't respect us as equals. According to them, the best-case scenario is harassment or racial profiling, and the worst-case is getting falsely accused or even shot. They reference the Rodney King and Sean Bell cases as proof.

Tonight we have to stop people at the gate because there's literally no room left in the courtyard. Since there's only a tall chain-link fence separating the party from the sidewalk, people start dancing right where they are. Of course I'm killing it on the 1s and 2s, so the crowd gets so big that the party spills into the street. After a while traffic can't get through.

I have to take a whiz, so I put on Jimmy Spicer's "Adventures of Super Rhymes" (remember, the thirteen-minute song?). That should give me enough time to get to the bathroom and back. I get one of my friends to watch my turntables to make sure nobody knocks over anything or steals any of my records.

The rec center is like a ghost town. You can hear the rowdy crowd outside, but no sound is coming from inside the center. Yancy and Carl must be out trying to control the people in the street. I don't know how they plan on doing that.

When I round the corner and head down the hallway to the bathrooms in the back, I hear voices.

"You can't fit all of that in there."

"Man, I got this. Relax."

There's a light on in the storage room and the door is ajar, so I peek in. Yancy and Carl are quickly gathering up rectangular packages full of white powder and giving them to Boo Boo, who is stashing them in his school backpack. He's the first one to see me, then Yancy. Carl is the last one to look up. None of us says a word. We're like four deer caught in the headlights of a speeding Hummer. I feel like all the water is sucked out of my body.

I turn around and walk outside with my eyes dried open. I haven't blinked. I even forget that I have to go to the bathroom.

As soon as I get back to my turntables, the cops show up. They disperse everybody without incident. Boo Boo leaves with the rest of the crowd. He has on his backpack and it's bulging. He stares at me as he's walking out and holds his glare until he's out of sight.

An officer approaches me and asks who's in charge. Yancy and Carl come out of the center as I point directly at them. I don't like how they look at me. While the cop goes to talk to them, I break down my equipment and bounce.

◈

I'm in the recording studio, and I'm having a hard time focusing on the music. I haven't seen Yancy and Carl since Friday, and today is Monday. They haven't called, and I know I'm going to have to holler at them eventually. I'm thinking I'll just do the block parties and mind my own business about the other stuff.

Boo Boo, on the other hand, is making a huge mistake. If he gets busted for being involved with drugs, he's going to do some serious time because of his prior convictions *and* because he's on probation. And since he got locked up that last time, he won't let me say two words to him.

When I think about it, how was Boo Boo supposed to turn out any other way? He's never had a real family, and the family he did have abused him, did him dirty, and then tossed him in the street like he was destined for the trash heap. Then Yancy and Carl step in, move him into their house when he gets out of Woodfield, and treat him like a son or a little brother. Boo Boo's never had nice clothes or felt important, but now they're lacing him with cash and credibility. I'm mad that I let Yancy and Carl fool me like they did, but I guess I shouldn't feel too bad because they have all of Mount Vernon hoodwinked.

Bang Up Black's whole crew is in the studio tonight with another pack of groupies. Now I understand why he was sniffing and all fidgety after he performed at the block party. Yancy and Carl took him into the center and laced him up like a pair of new Tims.

I don't know what Bang Up, his boys, and those groupies are doing in the back room, but it's like a party in there. I'm in the control room mixing down the song we just recorded.

Bang Up sticks his head out the door. "How much longer, son?"

"About fifteen more minutes."

"You good?"

"Yeah, I'm good."

"We got four bangers back here. You're welcome to partake if you like." His eyes are glazed over, and he has a silly grin on his face.

"Nah, I'm cool."

Something about the groupie thing doesn't seem right. I mean, how would I feel if I had a little sister who'd sleep with a guy just because he's famous? Or worse, what if my moms was like that? Not that I'm trying to be all righteous or anything, but those girls back there are just like Gessie and Shavonne. Would they even like me, Bang Up, or his crew if we weren't in the rap game?

Most guys don't care. They just take what they can get. But one thing's for sure, character doesn't count for much these days. If you have money and fame—even infamy—you'll have a fan base and the girls to go along with it.

I think about what the old man told me in church what seems like a lifetime ago, "All that glitters ain't gold." I don't know. It's a lot going on that I need to figure out.

I'm standing in front of a floor-length mirror in Winslow's Men's Wear on 4th Avenue. Mr. Lord is in the mirror beside me, showing me my assignment for the week. He noticed when I came to church that I never wore a necktie. I told him that I didn't even own one. He's buying me the untied tie I now have hanging around my neck because, according to him, "You can't call yourself a man if you don't know how to tie a tie."

Interesting concept.

"You also need to know how to tie the different knots because they each have a purpose depending on your mood, your outfit, or the occasion," he continues.

Learning how to tie six kinds of knots is going to be as hard as it was for me to figure out what I thought about absolute truth.

At first the idea of absolute truth didn't make sense. How can there be one truth that applies to everybody in every situation? When I wrote that down and turned it in, Mr. Lord pounced on it immediately.

He said, "So you don't think that truth can be absolute?"

"No," I said. I scrambled to figure out what booby trap of logic he was setting for me this time.

"Is what you just said absolutely true?"

"Yes."

"So you just stated an absolute truth."

Once I understood what he was saying, I realized he had a point. Absolute truth does exist. If it didn't, we wouldn't have a standard to base right or wrong on. That would mean anything goes, and that's just not how life works. If truth isn't absolute, then it's not truth. It's a choice. And if *that* was absolutely true, we'd be more confused than we already are.

I had to catch myself because I couldn't believe I was thinking like that. At that point I realized just how much Mr. Lord was rubbing off on me.

When Mr. Lord gave me this tie assignment, I thought he was taking it easy on me and giving me a break from the academic stuff. Right now he's showing me how to do a Windsor knot. The double-simple has already confused me three times, and I made a really big small knot twice. Now I'm just trying not to choke myself to death. I can see the headlines now: "Rap Producer Terror Tory strangles himself with a necktie in Winslow's." There'd be no way to spin that to make my death legendary like Biggie's or Tupac's.

Mr. Lord sees that I'm struggling. "Never lose your cool,"

he says. "You handicap your problem-solving ability when you do that."

As he's saying this, sweat is running from my armpits like an escaped convict.

"Let's start over," he says. "When frustration sets in, you become your own worst enemy."

I take a deep breath, calm myself, and start again. I keep a close eye on every twist and fold Mr. Lord makes with his tie as he walks me through the steps again.

He looks at me in the mirror. "You know, Tory, you're the closest thing I've ever had to a son."

I'm flattered that Mr. Lord said that, but it feels awkward at the same time. I've never had a close relationship with a man. I'm at a loss for words, but after a couple of uncomfortable moments, I ask the obvious question.

"Why didn't you just have more kids?"

"After Precious was born, we had a miscarriage and then we had a stillborn baby. So we decided to retire from the baby-making business."

"Oh. I'm sorry I asked about that."

"It's no problem. Do you want to hear something ironic?"

"What?"

"When I was growing up, my plan was to have two big-headed boys. So the first time Barbara got pregnant, I was so convinced that Eddie Junior was on the way that I was ready to skip the ultrasound appointment."

"Was Mrs. Lord cool with that?"

"Not at all. She felt it was a girl the whole time!"

We both laugh.

"I'm telling you, women's intuition is real." He gets serious again. "When the ultrasound showed that we were having a girl, it took me awhile to get over it. But when Precious was born, I was so overwhelmed at how precious she was that we decided to name her that."

"So you didn't name her after the song?"

"No, we didn't make that connection until after we had already filled out the birth certificate. That was a good thing because had we thought about it, we probably would've chosen a different name. Neither of us was into the God thing back then."

"Really? What made you change?"

Mr. Lord thinks about it for a moment. "Pain and disappointment. The miscarriage and the stillbirth made us realize that there were things in our lives that were beyond our control. And we wondered where our babies were, so we had to figure out what we thought about life and death. In order for us to make sense of the loss, we had to accept that there was more to the life experience than what takes place on earth. Obviously, we didn't change overnight, but that was what started us on the path of trying to figure out what the God thing was all about."

With that, my Windsor knot falls right into place.

"See what happens when you keep your cool?" he says.

I think of how cool it would be to have a dad to teach you things. Mr. Lord is the closest thing I've ever had to a father.

My moms never said how long these weekly meetings

have to continue, but I've started to look forward to talking to Mr. Lord each week.

"All six knots, let's hear them," he says.

"The Windsor, the half-Windsor, the double-simple, the small knot, the four-in-hand, and . . ." I'm racking my brain to remember the sixth one.

"Think Christ," he says.

"Right, the cross knot."

"Good. So now that you've seen me do each one a couple of times, you should be able to figure them out by yourself, right?"

"I should be able to." I sound more confident than I am.

"How many suits do you have?"

"Four."

He picks out three more ties and takes them to the register. "I'll start you off with one for each suit. Then you can build your own collection from there."

The lady at the register smiles as she rings us up. "Nothing like seeing a father raising his son."

Neither of us correct her.

On the ride home from Winslow's, I have a ton of questions bouncing around inside of my head, from the Rapfest experience to Bang Up Black to Yancy and Carl. But it's the life-and-death question that has been with me for as long as I can remember. The conversation in the store gives me the perfect opportunity to get Mr. Lord's take on where all the dead people go, especially my dad.

"What do you think happens after you die?"

"Interesting way to phrase the question," Mr. Lord says.

"What do you mean?"

"You said what do I *think* happens after death."

"That's because nobody can know for sure. The only people who know aren't coming back."

"Hindus who believe in reincarnation would disagree with you, and so would people with a biblical world-view."

I don't get rattled when I talk to Mr. Lord anymore because I know he's only trying to get me to "think critically and be accountable" for what I believe.

"So what do you think?" I ask him again.

"We all die once, and after that we're judged for everything we did on earth."

"Judged by God?"

"Right."

"But that's just your religious belief," I say.

"And so is everybody's belief about what happens after death."

"Not the person who doesn't believe in God."

"Not true. Religion is just a set of beliefs that a person thinks are true based on their faith in them. If someone thinks there's no life after death, or even if they think there's no God at all, they have faith that what they're saying is true. But apart from some reasonable explanation based on something other than their feelings, they can't know for sure what happens after death."

"So how can you be so sure that what you believe is true?" I ask.

"Because I personally know someone who was dead three days and then came back to life."

"For real? Who?" I say, completely engrossed.

"Think cross knot."

"Oh," I say. "You're talking about Jesus. I thought you were going to tell me about somebody I could actually talk to."

"He only talks to people who are interested in truth. He created the universe, so he's not going to be anybody's side project."

He's spreading it on a little thick, if you ask me. And none of what he's saying tells me where my dad is right now.

We ride the rest of the way home in silence.

When we pull up in front of the house, Mr. Lord turns to me once more. "Do you know where the most reliable ancient historical documents can be found?"

"The Bible?" I say this not because I believe it, but because I know that's where he's going. I've been around him long enough to recognize when he's using a question to set up a point.

"Specifically, the New Testament," he says, "which contains four biographies about Jesus written by some of his closest friends and followers. Everything they wrote down they either witnessed themselves or interviewed someone who witnessed it. But don't take my word for it. Look it up yourself. As a matter of fact, write down every reason you think that makes the Bible false or unreliable. Then we'll discuss it."

"I thought tying the knots was my next assignment."

Mr. Lord holds up the bag and smiles. "To whom much is given, much is required."

When I get in the house, Moms is in the kitchen cooking dinner. I know she's going to be amped when she sees my four new ties.

"Yancy and Carl just left," she says. "I'm surprised you didn't see them. They literally just walked out the door."

That cold sensation of fear washes over me again. "Did they say what they came for?"

"The block parties. They're not going to be doing them anymore because they've gotten too big. They wanted you to call them as soon as you got in."

I go to my room, but I don't call. The thought of Yancy and Carl sitting in my living room talking to my moms makes my stomach knot up. It seems like one of those intimidation tactics you see in old movies like *Scarface* or *The Godfather*. And nobody would even believe me if I told them Yancy and Carl were dealing drugs. They even have the mayor fooled—he came to the ribbon-cutting ceremony when they first opened the center back in May. But since they're not having any more block parties, there's no real reason for me to call them back.

Today is my first music video shoot. We're doing the video for "Street Theater," and it's going to be directed by Benny Boom, one of the most creative video directors in the game. "Street Theater" wasn't officially released until a full month after it had been playing on our station as a Power 97 exclusive. By the time radio stations in the rest of the country started playing it, it was the official summer anthem of New York.

Magic says, "I did it that way because I'm not interested in just growing the label, I want to generate buzz and ratings for the radio station at the same time. Then we all benefit—the station, my artists, and Magic Music. That's what you call good business, creating a win-win situation for everyone you're in partnership with."

I'm learning a lot from Magic about how the industry works. I used to think it was only about making the hottest beats, but he's showing me the importance of advertising, sales, marketing, publishing, and publicity.

Here's an example. The video is going to require hundreds of extras for the street scenes, so we've been talking about the shoot on the air for the last couple of weeks. But that's about way more than extras. We're letting everybody across the country know that a video for the song is coming soon, which generates searches and discussions on Twitter, Facebook, Google, YouTube, MySpaceTV, and all the hip-hop websites and blogs. That kind of buzz will get you on MTV when the video comes out. Once you're on MTV, you're officially a crossover hit because the few videos they play these days are only for the biggest artists. Then you politic that into getting the song played in arenas during professional sports games, in commercials, and in highlight reels on the sports channels. Magic has a saying that "buzz and blogs are how stars are made and paid in the Internet age."

The video is going to be shot in Bang Up Black's neighborhood in Harlem, and the concept is funny fresh. The idea presents Harlem at night as a reality show, with Bang Up Black as the host. He'll be riding around in a tricked-out Hummer capturing all the "street theater" you find in his hood at night. His camera crew is going to be Harlem's three biggest rappers, Cam'ron, Juelz Santana, and Jim Jones. The opening shot will show the sun setting behind the Harlem skyline in time-release photography. Everything else will take place after dark.

I'm not going to be in the reality-show part of the video. All of my scenes will take place on top of the Harlem Stage Gatehouse, an old castle-like building that's one of the highest points in Manhattan. Benny Boom is going to shoot my scenes first so I can be in the car heading home by midnight. (Moms gave me an extra hour on my recording studio curfew since it's a night shoot.) In one scene I'll be cutting it up on the 1s and 2s with choreographed dancers behind me, and in another scene I'll be making a beat on an MPC surrounded by eight-foot speakers.

The view of the city from that high up at night is straight bonkers. Benny said he's going to use wide-angle lenses and a crane to swing around and catch me at a bunch of different angles. Then he's going to intercut my scenes throughout the video.

I called up Baron (X Wretch), and he agreed to come through and be my chaperone since Corey's out of town at a math competition and Devin is starring in a play. Baron's from Harlem, and Moms met him at a barbeque at the Lords' house a few weeks after Rapfest. She thinks he's cool, so the chaperone thing is all square.

My call time is 5:30 p.m. on the corner of 145th and

Broadway. When I pull up, Baron is already there talking to Bang Up Black and his crew.

"Y'all know each other?" I ask.

Bang Up is high, so he's extra hyped. "No doubt, me and this dude go all the way back to elementary school. Before he got all religious, we used to run this corner. He *was* nicer than me on the mike until he started rapping for J-J-J-Jesus." Bang Up stutters the name to maximize the diss, but Baron doesn't take it lightly.

> I'll destroy you with truth and still keep it Christ
>   in the booth.
> And we can get it on right here unless you strug-
>   gling with fear.
> Bang Up Black. You talk a lot of smack in your
>   raps.
> But I'll take your life—to the throne of grace—and
>   pray that God shuts your trap.
> My freestyle is still sick. Just like your soul.
> And even though we been down since we was five
>   years old? I'm sold
> As a slave in the kingdom of God.
> Call it what you want, son. But I'm done being
>   hard.

The whole corner shouts, "Ohhhhhhh!" Baron and Bang Up slap five and hug.

"I still love you, man," Baron says. "And I'm praying for you."

Bang Up actually looks moved. "Love you too, bro. And I appreciate the prayers, for real."

Seeing all the production trucks and crew people lining the street gives me goose bumps. Remember when I told you at the beginning of the sTory that I was going to be the man? Well, I thought I was the man after I did my first show on Power and I stepped into Times Square, where my car service was waiting. But now with my own trailer? On the set of a music video? And we have the number one song in the country? Now I'm *really* the man.

My trailer has everything in it I asked for. Last week I had to fill out something called a rider that lets the video production people know what you want in your trailer during the shoot. I'm enjoying getting all this free stuff. I got bottled water, a couple of Rip It energy drinks, some Veggie Booties, and granola.

Baron takes one of the Rip Its and pops the top. "One of my dudes in Iraq told me this is what they drink over there." He picks through my snacks. "You ain't got nothing unhealthy in here, like Fudge Rounds or Cheetos or something?"

"Nah, this stuff tastes better." I'm surprised he even eats junk food since he's built like the Incredible Hulk. "I didn't know you and Bang Up Black were that tight."

"Yeah, we had a crew back in the day. He was always more serious about rapping than I was. I was into a bunch of dumb stuff that didn't have nothing to do with rap."

"So what happened? You're like a thugged-out Jesus dude now."

Baron pulls up his shirt and shows me a nasty scar across his chest. "I was lying in the street probably ten feet from where this trailer is," he says. "A dude I'd stuck

165

up a couple of hours earlier came back and shot me at point-blank range. I kid you not, it felt like my whole chest exploded. The bullet bounced around my chest cavity like a basketball. It fractured one of my ribs and tore up the lining of my left lung.

"I got shot on the sidewalk, but the force of the blast knocked me into the street. It was winter, and the asphalt was frozen. I still remember the feeling of warm blood oozing down my chest, flowing around to my back, and completely soaking the back of my shirt."

Hearing Baron describe getting shot with this amount of detail is crazy riveting. It's like a gangsta rap record come to life.

"So I have this flaming, open wound in my chest, and then I feel my left lung starting to collapse. After that, every breath I took felt like I was getting stabbed with an ice pick. It was worse than suffocating because you don't want to breathe since it hurts so bad. But you can only hold your breath for so long. Then I started losing my vision 'cuz I was losing so much blood. After a while I couldn't see anything. I could just hear the hysteria on the street.

"So I'm laying there feeling my life gushing out of me. I'd heard about Allah, Buddha, and all these other gods, but for some reason I said, 'Yo, Jesus'—and I wasn't trying to be disrespectful, that's just how street I was back then. So I said, 'Yo, Jesus, if you're real you can save me,' because at that point I was leaving this world and I knew it. To this day I don't know how I got to the hospital, but you know what still bugs me out?"

"What?" I answer, on the edge of my seat.

"When I got to the hospital, I got robbed by one of the nurses. I guess she took one look at me and knew I wasn't going to make it, so she took my Rolex and the $600 I had in my wallet. But since I stole all of that from somebody else, I was just reaping what I'd sown."

"You got robbed by a nurse in the emergency room?"

"For real," Baron says. "But the worst pain hadn't even happened yet. They had to use this saw to cut open my chest and put a tube in to drain fluid off my lungs. Then they had to give me what they called positive pressure. I don't know how they call anything with that much pain positive. They had to bear down on my chest, and when they did, it forced this reddish-brown fluid out of my chest cavity. That had to be the worst pain I ever felt in my life."

"You were conscious while they were doing all of that?"

"They thought I was unconscious, and maybe I was, but I could feel everything. And right in the middle of them doing all of that, I flatlined right on the table. They tried to revive me for a few minutes, but after they couldn't, they unhooked me from all the machines and everything. After everybody left the room, I started breathing on my own.

"So when you hear people say Jesus saves, I know it's true, and I'm not talking about no religious experience. He raised me from the dead, for real."

Now that's street theater.

Our conversation is cut short when one of the film crew

knocks on the door and tells me it's time to shoot my first scene. I didn't even get a chance to ask Baron about the scar on his face.

Once I'm on the set, Reality climbs up on my shoulders, and his partner, Intimidation, whispers in my ear that I'm the only teenager out here. My first shot is supposed to be me cutting and scratching, simple stuff I've done a million times in my life. But after ten or eleven takes, we still don't have anything usable because I keep messing up. It's hard to relax and just do *me* with all the lights, the crew people, and the dancers behind me.

The more takes I blow, the more frustrated I get. I remember Mr. Lord saying that when frustration sets in, you become your own worst enemy. Right now me and myself are in World War III. Benny Boom remains calm, but I feel like everybody else is looking at me thinking I don't belong here.

Magic comes over and pulls me to the side. He doesn't look mad, but he doesn't look happy either. He says, "Tory, we're going to do this one more time, and you're going to get it right." He walks away.

Something about the way he says it gets to me. When Benny calls "Action!" I start cutting it up like I'm Funkmaster Flex, DJ Drama, and DJ Clue all wrapped in one. I scratch with my chin, my elbow, and my pointer finger. Then I spin around and scratch behind my back.

I hear Benny call "Cut!" but I'm so wound up from being embarrassed and mad at myself that I keep going. He shouts, "Roll camera, roll camera!"

I go on for another couple of minutes before I finally stop. The set goes wild. Terror Tory's now in the building (even though we're outside). Now I feel like I belong up in here.

Me and Baron walk back to my trailer while the next scene is being lit. An Accord rolls up, and Yancy and Carl hop out.

"What up, Tory?" Carl says. "Where've you been? We've been trying to catch you."

"I've been busy. My moms told me y'all are deading the block parties. I figured that's all you wanted to talk to me about."

"Let's talk business for a minute," Yancy says. "Get in."

They must be crazy if they think I'm getting in the car with them. I'm not as stupid as I look.

"That's alright. I'm shooting right now."

I can tell Carl is getting annoyed, and he's not doing a good job of hiding it. "We're just going around the block. Hop in."

Baron steps forward and extends his hand to shake. "Hi you doing? I'm Baron."

Carl looks at Baron's hand like it's covered in hock spit. Baron then offers his hand to Yancy. "Baron," he says. Yancy leaves him hanging too.

Baron shrugs and continues, "Tory's not getting in the car with you. And anything you want to say to him, you're gonna have to say with me standing right here." Baron looks at me. "That cool?"

I nod.

Yancy and Carl step closer to Baron. "See that car right there?" Yancy says. "We're going to get in it. With Tory. And we're going to discuss a private matter that doesn't concern you."

Carl moves toward me, but Baron blocks his way. Carl shakes his head with fire in his eyes. "My man, you don't know me."

"I don't. But what I do know is this conversation's over. I don't know where you from, but this is my hood. And it wouldn't be a good idea for you to act up out here. Everybody's not as nice as me."

Baron grabs my arm, and we start walking to the trailer. Baron doesn't look back. I turn around and see Carl and Yancy frozen in place.

Once we're in the trailer, Baron looks at me. "Why they coming at you like that?"

"If I tell you, you have to promise me you won't tell anybody."

"I don't make those kinds of promises. But I can promise you this, whatever that situation is, it's not going away. Those dudes are mad sheisty. I can smell the hustle on 'em."

I should be celebrating shooting my first music video, but all I can think about is Yancy and Carl. What would they have done if I'd gotten in that car?

◆

On Sunday I'm sitting in front of Mr. Lord, and he's going over my list. On almost every one, he nods his head or goes, "Yeah, good one."

When he's finished reading, he looks up. "I would call

these 'the skeptic's greatest hits.' Every one of these tripped me up at some point too. Let's go over them."

He slides my paper back to me. Mr. Lord has to be one of the smoothest dudes I know. Here I am about to fire these questions at him, and he's sitting there cool as a purple Popsicle.

I start with the first point. "The Bible has been translated too many times to know what it really said when it was first written. You ever played that telephone game?"

"The one where you give a message to a person and they whisper it to the next person, and by the time it gets to the last person, it's a totally different message?"

"Yeah, that's just like the Bible," I say, pleased at how well this is starting off.

"Actually, it's very different for a number of reasons. Let's look at the New Testament, for example. It's not a typical book. It's twenty-seven different documents written by nine different people over a twenty- to fifty-year period and then collected into a single volume. It's not just made-up stories passed down by one person telling it to someone else. These individuals actually witnessed the events they wrote about or interviewed someone who did. So what was passed down was eyewitness testimony."

"But how do we know they weren't just making up stuff to create a religion?"

"Do you realize that all of the disciples except one were killed for their beliefs? Would you make up a story and then go around telling people it's true if you knew it was going to get you killed?"

"Maybe they didn't know it was going to get them killed."

"Tory, this happened in the Roman Empire. To believe in any other god besides Caesar was illegal. That's one of the reasons they were killed."

I'm still not convinced, but I'll move on. I know he won't be able to get out of this next one.

"What about this? It's not possible for somebody to come back from the dead."

Mr. Lord laughs. "Of course it's not possible. That's why it's called a miracle. Let me ask you a question."

"Okay."

"If a member of Mount Vernon City Council bought a gravesite and gave it to you, wouldn't it be easy to find out where you were buried, even hundreds of years from now?"

"I guess so."

"And if he had two Mount Vernon cops guard your grave after you died to make sure nobody dug you up, couldn't we safely say that it would be almost impossible for anyone to move your dead body?"

"Yes, but what does that have to do with Jesus?"

"Everything. The person who gave Jesus his tomb was a real person who was a member of the Sanhedrin, which was like a religious governing body. Two Roman soldiers were assigned to guard Jesus's tomb because when he was killed, it was a major political event in Jerusalem. Even non-Christian books tell you that. On the third day after he was killed, nobody denied the tomb was empty. The Sanhedrin just said the disciples had stolen the body."

"Maybe they did."

"Tory, the disciples were in hiding after Jesus was killed because they didn't know if they were going to be next. But even if they weren't running for their lives, they were poor common people, not soldiers. Roman soldiers were the best trained in the world at that time. And Caesar had a policy that any soldier who allowed someone he was guarding to escape would be executed. Wouldn't you be on extra alert knowing it would cost you your life if someone you were guarding got away?"

"But the Bible was written hundreds of years after Jesus died," I say.

"Says who?"

I don't say anything because I don't know who said it.

"The earliest New Testament writings that archaeologists have found were written about thirty years after Jesus lived. When you compare those early copies to what we have today, you see that there's hardly any difference in content. And you know hip-hop artists from thirty years ago, and you weren't even born yet. If you wrote a book today that said that Grandmaster Flash performed miracles and raised people from the dead at block parties in 1979, it would never fly. Do you know why?"

"Why?"

"Because there are too many people still alive who were there who would say it didn't happen. So a global religious movement based on your story would never start. And the birth of Christianity was a lot more controversial than the birth of hip-hop."

"But what about all the contradictions in the Bible?"

"Which ones?"

"I mean, I don't know what they are, I've just heard about them."

"This isn't some trick I'm trying to play on you, Tory. When you buy a piece of musical equipment, you do all kinds of research before you choose which one you're going to buy, right?"

"Right."

"So if you spend that much time researching something like musical equipment, wouldn't it make sense to spend at least that much time researching whether or not the Bible is true?"

Mr. Lord has a point, but I'm not ready to deal with all of this stuff right now. The truth is, I'm fine with my life the way it is. I'm not hurting anybody. I'm basically a good person, and I do what makes me feel good. I can worry about this religion stuff when I get older. And you know what? Even if the Bible is true, that doesn't mean I want to do everything that's in it.

17

Ever since we wrapped shooting the video, Magic has been telling me and Bang Up to come up with ideas for the next single. That's why I'm in the crib now, chopping up Javanese Gamelan music and feeding it to my sampler. I bought a record called "Udan Mas" at Vinyl Village on 3rd Street. I'd never even heard of Javanese Gamelan music, and that's exactly why I bought it. The more obscure the music genre, the less likely people will recognize your sample. And I'm on to something tonight because what I'm coming up with sounds as chaotic and funky as one of those Public Enemy tracks produced by The Bomb Squad.

I have the music cranked up so loud that Moms startles me when she jabs me in the back with the telephone. I didn't hear it ringing or her coming into the room.

"Turn that music *down*," she says.

"Okay, sorry. Hello?"

"Tory, it's Magic."

"And Bang Up Black. We got you on three-way. Sounds like your moms is bugging out."

"Nah, she's cool," I say.

"What are you cooking up over there?" Magic asks.

"I have some Indonesian music in the pot."

"Word?"

"Yeah, it's all percussion, cymbals, and bells and stuff."

"That's good you're flipping it like that because I got a game-changing idea for the next single," Bang Up says.

"Let's hear it," Magic says.

"Nah, I want to keep it under wraps until we get to the studio."

"Well, it better be nice since you're imposing gag orders on yourself," Magic says. "And tomorrow we're going to meet at the editing suite before we hit the studio. Benny has a final cut of the video he wants us to see."

I stay up pretty late putting the finishing touches on the track since Bang Up is making such a big deal out of his idea. As a producer you never want an emcee's lyrics to outshine your beats.

When I finally hit the sack, I can't sleep. I'm amped about seeing the video tomorrow. It feels like Christmas Eve and my favorite toy is waiting for me under the tree.

When we get to the editing suite, the only ones there are me, Magic, Bang Up, Benny Boom, Cazzie the video editor, and the president of Vantage Records. When the lights go down and the countdown on the big screen starts, I get the feeling you have when you're climbing to the top of a roller coaster. When the video starts rolling, we're going down a hundred miles an hour. Even though I had read the music video treatment, seen the story-boards, and asked Benny a bunch of questions, nothing could have prepared me for the heat that I'm seeing on the screen right now.

When it's over, everybody is speechless. After a couple of moments of silence, we all let out our breath at the same time. The video is unbelievable. It makes me look like I'm a real hip-hop artist.

Even though this magic carpet ride has been going on for a few months now, I still see myself as the same person. But seeing myself in the video is like watching someone cool who I want to be like. The colors, the shots, the lighting—I've never seen anything like it. The craziest part is that Benny was running the camera at times when I didn't know it. He has these moments when I'm looking straight into the lens or off into space, but it looks hot. Like it was planned.

Bang Up is hyped too. He looks cooler than me in the video, but he's supposed to. He's older and he's the artist.

This video should win some awards.

Magic and the president of Vantage shake hands and look at each other like they just stole something valuable and no one knows about it yet. Magic is trying to play it cool, but I can see that he's proud that his idea of putting me and Bang Up together is paying off so well.

On the two-block walk to the recording studio, the three of us don't say anything. I think the video stunned us into thinking about the possibilities that lie ahead. It's one thing to hear the song on the radio, even when it's number one (which it has been for the last three weeks), but the power of the visual image takes the song to another level.

Bang Up's crew and a new set of groupies are waiting for us in the lobby of the studio when we get there. Magic tells them to wait outside for a minute while he takes us inside. He looks mad serious. So serious that me and Bang Up look at each other, concerned.

"I wanted to wait until we got in the studio before I broke this to you," Magic says. He pulls the two rolling chairs from under the mixing board. "You should probably sit down."

We both do. He couldn't have anything bad to say because we just saw the video, and he was as excited about it as we were. And he started telling us over a week ago to come up with ideas for a new single.

Magic takes a big sigh and starts to speak. "We've had a great run, and we've worked well together as a team so far. But having this much success so quickly demands that we do something that wasn't originally a part of the plan." Magic drops his head and takes a deep breath. He looks back up. "I don't know how to break this to you, but you two have the misfortune of headlining Summer Fest."

Me and Bang Up jump out of our seats, bump chests, and high-five each other like we just won the Super Bowl. Truthfully, being in Summer Fest (even if you're not headlining) is like winning the Super Bowl. Summer Fest is THE concert series of the summer. Last year 55,000 people packed Yankee Stadium for it. The lineup is always who-ever has the biggest hits of the summer. There are also tons of guest appearances from anybody who's anybody in hip-hop and R & B. You never know who's going show up because if you're a star, it's the place to be in August.

I have to sit down again because I really can't believe this is happening. By now Bang Up has brought in his en-tourage, and it's straight mania in here. They're all trying to lift me out of my seat to celebrate with them, but I'm so overwhelmed I just want to sit. Summer Fest? Head-lining? This is too good to be true.

Bang Up quiets everybody and tells us what his "game-changing idea" is. He wants to do a remake of James Brown's "Sex Machine." I'm not really feeling that because I don't like to sample records that are that popular. From the look on Magic's face, he's not feeling it either.

Bang Up catches on and starts to explain. "I don't want to do a literal remake. I just want to use the name and the concept because it's a song that everybody knows."

"Oh, okay," Magic says, "because James Brown samples went out with Jheri Curls and fat shoelaces."

Up until this point Bang Up's rhymes haven't been crazy at all because he mostly talks about his rhyming skills using clever wordplay. What's ironic is that as much as he curses in real life, he doesn't use any curse words in his rhymes.

I load up the new track. "You got the lyrics already?" I ask.

"Nah, just the idea. You know I like to write to the track. Let me hear what you got for me."

I crafted a sinister-sounding beat around the Gamelan sample. It has a raging drum track, a vibrating bass line, and some horn licks that I recorded off a video game. I filtered the high- and low-end frequencies out of the horns to give them a tinny, stabbing sound. Then I split the horns onto two tracks and panned them left and right for a stereo effect.

As soon as the beat comes on, the groupies start doing that sexy reggaeton dancing, rotating their hips around like they're bouncing on a string. Bang Up's boys get up on them like they're at a dark, smoky basement party. That means the beat is working.

Bang Up drops into his seat, tunes everybody out, and starts writing lyrics on his yellow legal pad. After a couple of minutes, he looks up at me.

"We gonna go in the back and set it off right quick. I'm gonna be ready to lay something down in a minute. Pump up the music in my room."

Bang Up, his crew, and the girls pile into the back while I keep working on the track. Each time I add something new, I hear muffled applause filter out of the back room. Magic is seated beside me at the mixing board bobbing his head as I construct the beat piece by piece.

It just so happens that I have the "Sex Machine" record with me. I like to cut up the "Huh!" that James Brown does one minute into the song.

While I'm recording some cuts and scratches to the beat, Bang Up sticks his head out of the room. He's glassy-eyed and wearing that silly grin again. "Yo, Tory, run a mike back here so you can record me getting my thing on for the track. I want everything to be real on this next single."

Is he serious? He actually wants me to record him doing the wild thing and put it in my beat? Moms's words pierce my skull and gnaw at my brain like a hundred-pound Rottweiler: "You have to be very careful what you allow on top of your tracks."

Now I'm face-to-face with a decision. I stop the music.

"I'm not putting that in the track," I say, barely loud enough to be heard.

Bang Up's crew and the groupies peek out of the back room to see what he's going to do.

"What did you say?" Bang Up demands, a mix of anger and embarrassment taking over his skinny face.

This moment feels like it's suspended in time. I think about *character* (firmness blended with judgment) and *integrity* (uncompromising adherence to an artistic code). If I don't do what Bang Up is asking me to do, I'll look like the scared little boy in hip-hop. If I do it, I'll be going against what my conscience says is right.

I take off my headphones and force myself to answer louder, even though I'm intimidated by the pressure and all the eyes.

"I said I'm not putting that in my music."

Magic says, "Yo, Bang Up, you gotta take the sexcapades somewhere else, man."

Bang Up ignores Magic and directs all his fury at me. "Check this out—you're fired! I don't want no square heads corrupting my craft!"

Suddenly three men rush into the studio, flashing badges. One of them says, "DEA!"

"You're busting in a recording session," Magic says. "I need to see a warrant."

The agent jabs a piece of paper in Magic's face. "Can you read that?" He spins me around and handcuffs me. "You're under arrest." He reads me my rights as he gives the cuffs an extra-tight squeeze.

◆

The ride to Mount Vernon from the city is quick because the DEA agents have their sirens and lights flashing like I'm Frank Lucas or somebody. I know I didn't do anything, but I'm getting scared. Once you get caught up in the justice system, getting justice can be a crapshoot. I mean, look at what's happening right now. Bang Up and his entourage had the drugs in the studio, but I'm the one wearing the bracelets. I don't even know what I'm getting arrested for.

When we get to the police station, they hustle me into an interrogation room. A tough-looking agent who could easily pass for a drill sergeant comes in wearing a scowl instead of military fatigues.

"You're going to do a whole lot of time for this, you know that, right?"

I don't say anything.

"Running coke for your boys?" He sucks his teeth and shakes his head. "Juries don't take too kindly to that kind of stuff."

"I didn't do anything," I say.

"That's not what Yancy and Carl said. They said you got them new business from your new rapper friends."

He throws a stack of photos on the table and slams the door as he walks out. I don't touch the pictures, but I can see most of them because of the way they're spread across the table. There are pictures of me deejaying at the block parties. There are also pictures of Bang Up the night he performed. Do they know he was in the center doing coke that night? Are Yancy and Carl trying to protect Boo Boo by pinning this on me?

My hands start to tremble. Aren't they supposed to take these cuffs off?

I'm shook right now, but I'm not going to look scared. That'll make them think I have something to be scared about.

I knew everything was too good to be true. Now I'm sitting here in the police station with the DEA accusing me of being a drug runner. I've heard about innocent people pleading guilty to lesser charges to avoid a maximum sentence. Is that what's going to happen to me?

The door opens, and Moms and her boss, Mr. Lufkin, come in. Moms hugs me and kisses me on the head.

Mr. Lufkin takes charge. I don't think the feds expected someone like me to have a partner from Lufkin, Kravitz, and Klume show up.

"This arrest and interrogation has lawsuit written all over it," Mr. Lufkin says. "Take those handcuffs off my client."

The bracelets are quickly removed. Mr. Lufkin turns to me. "Did they ask you anything?"

"Yes."

Mr. Lufkin glares at the drill sergeant when he comes back in. "He's sixteen. Do you know the law as it relates to the interrogation of minors?"

The agent doesn't say anything.

Mr. Lufkin asks again, "Sir, are you aware of the law as it relates to the interrogation of minors?"

The agent's face hardens. "I'm a federal agent. I know the law."

"Great. You are now free to legally question my client in the presence of his legal counsel and his mother."

The agent folds his muscular arms but remains silent.

"Are you arresting him?" Mr. Lufkin asks.

"No, we're not."

"So if you don't have enough evidence to hold my client, and if there are no further questions, we'll be leaving."

When I walk out of the interrogation room, Yancy and Carl are sitting outside with their hands cuffed behind their backs. If looks could kill, I would have been dead before we made eye contact. I feel their eyes burning a hole in my back as we walk out of the station.

We step out of the building, and flashes from news cameras go off like fireworks. It's like TV with reporters shouting questions at us as we get into the cab. The main thing on my mind is what Precious is going to think when she hears about this.

The next morning the story is on the front page of the *Mount Vernon Enquirer* and the *Journal News*, in the gossip section of the *New York Daily News*, on Page Six in the *New York Post*, and in the music section of the *New York Times*. None of the articles are long, but they all say the same thing. "Power 97 DJ and rapper Terror Tory arrested in federal drug investigation."

First of all, I don't rap, I produce, and second of all, the headline makes it seem like I'm guilty. The hip-hop websites and blogs even interviewed some of the groupies who were in the studio. But they don't know anything because they were in the room in the back of the vocal booth where you can only hear if the talkback button is depressed.

Why is everybody so worried about what happens to me anyway? Because I produced one number one record, that means the whole truth doesn't need to be said about me? I didn't even do anything, but I guarantee you my character and integrity are going to take a hit because of this.

18

On Sunday I don't want to go to church because I'm not up to dealing with stares or questions. Moms picks up on how I'm feeling when she enters the room.

"Tory, you don't have anything to be ashamed of."

"I know that, Moms. But how many people are going to think I'm a drug dealer now?"

She sighs because she's the one who taught me that bad news travels faster than good news, even when it's not true. This whole media spotlight thing is new to both of us.

"I just want to stay home," I say.

"Then I'll stay here with you."

Around one o'clock, there's a knock at the door. I check to see who it is before I open it. I'm still a little spooked by the way Yancy and Carl looked at me when I left the police station. I don't know how big their operation is, but it has to be more than a few street dealers if the feds are involved. Mr. Lufkin says the agents intentionally walked me out in front of them to make it look like I was talking. He called it a classic case of divide and conquer. And even though I didn't say anything, it looks like I did. Those tactics might work for the feds, but that's the kind of stuff that gets you killed in the hood.

It's Precious and Mr. and Mrs. Lord at the door. When I let them in, Precious gives me a big hug. I have to remember this date because this'll go down in hisTory as our official first embrace. Mr. Lord hugs me next, and then Mrs. Lord. None of them say anything, they just sit. Those hugs let me know they don't think I'm a drug dealer. That's because they know the real me, not the "Power 97 DJ and rapper Terror Tory arrested in federal drug investigation."

Mr. Lord speaks first. "We thought you could use some support, so we decided to stop by."

"We really appreciate it," Moms says.

"We know you didn't do anything, Tory," Precious says with a little attitude.

I'm smiling on the inside because her swag is cute. Now I know I have her support.

Mr. Lord looks around. "Where's Corey and Devin?"

"At work."

"You two up to riding to the Hudson Valley with us? We're going apple picking in Newburgh."

Moms looks at me to see if I'm down.

"Let's do it," I say. "Getting away from here would be nice."

As we're driving up the New York State Thruway, I'm amazed at how different it is up here from where I live.

There are mountains, wilderness, and deer grazing right beside the highway. I count at least six dead deer on the side of the road. I guess those signs telling you to watch out for deer for the next thirty-two miles aren't doing a good job of protecting Bambi and his friends.

I also see a bunch of large birds circling overhead. Mr. Lord says they're vultures. I hope that's not some kind of sign. We pass a flock of them eating something dead in a field, and they look like ugly turkeys. Bambi and flying turkeys—they don't have that kind of stuff in Mount Vernon.

Precious turns to me. "So, how are you doing?"

"I'm alright."

"You nervous?"

"A little bit."

"You want to talk about it?"

"Okay."

We ride for a moment in silence. She gives me that "so go ahead and talk" look. I guess I don't have anything to say.

"Well . . . I wanted you to have this," Precious says. She hands me something wrapped in tissue paper. "I made it myself," she says shyly.

It's a pearl-white 5 x 7 picture frame. Inside the frame is a piece of textured paper that looks like a clear blue sky. It has white words typed on it in a cursive font: *God is our refuge and strength, a very present help in trouble.*

"That's Psalm 46:1," she says. "It's appropriate given the circumstances, don't you think?"

"Thanks."

Our first gift exchange, and I don't have anything to give her. I wonder if picture frames with Bible verses will be to me and her what pepperoni pizza with extra cheese was to Moms and Dad. Does this mean she likes me?

When we get back from apple picking, Magic is parked in front of the house. I realize that my short vacation from all the drama in my life is over. I don't have a problem with Magic, but seeing his truck makes me think about Bang Up and his drugs and groupies, the news reports, and the possibility of getting sent away to Woodfield for something I didn't do. Basically, it's my word against Yancy and Carl's, but it's two of them and only one of me.

Magic has a DVD of the music video for us. I'm not as amped about it as I was before all the drama hit the fan.

The Lords come inside to watch it. Seeing the video on our little TV is nothing like watching it on the big screen at the editing suite, but Moms and Mr. and Mrs. Lord are still blown away.

I look over at Precious. She smiles. "That was *real* nice, Tory. You actually look cute on there."

Everybody cracks up, but I'm on cloud nine plus nine. All the drugs and alcohol in the world couldn't get me as high as I am right now. Precious Lord called me cute.

◆

On Monday I'm back at the recording studio. Bang Up is surfing the Web on the control-room computer. Amazingly, he's by himself and clear-eyed. As soon as he sees me, he grins and slaps me five so hard it makes my hand hot. I'm relieved because I thought he was still going to be mad about the "Sex Machine" thing.

"Son, you're the most googled person in hip-hop right now! And it's good to know you ain't a snitch. I thought the feds were coming for us when they busted up in here. What you into, man? You supposed to be Mr. Squeaky Clean."

"I'm not into anything."

"Even if you're not, in hip-hop there's no such thing as bad publicity."

Bang Up continues to grin as he clicks away on the computer. I can't believe he actually thinks me getting arrested is a good thing.

"And it's perfect timing too," he continues. "We got the number one single in the country, the video drops this week, we're headlining Summer Fest on Saturday, and the album drops next month. Yo, look at this!"

He's on the TMZ home page. They have a picture of me in handcuffs being placed in the car. Somebody must've taken it with a camera phone because I don't remember seeing any photographers when I was led out of the studio.

Magic comes in and Bang Up calls to him. "Yo, Maj, check this out!"

Magic looks at the computer and then at me. He sees that I'm boiling. I feel like knocking Bang Up out right now. This is all a joke to him.

I yank the plug out of the wall, and the monitor goes black.

Bang Up's eyes narrow into slits. "Didn't you see me looking at that?"

"Do you even know what character is?"

"You think I'm stupid? Somebody in a movie or TV show."

"I'm talking about judgment, self-discipline, having a good reputation."

Bang Up jumps in my face. "This is hip-hop. Ain't nobody checking for that."

Magic gets between us. "Y'all need to chill. We have a show in five days. I'm not going to look stupid hosting it and have my artists' performance be wack because of some bickering."

"I don't even want to be on the same stage with this little punk!" Bang Up says.

"Maybe if you had some integrity, we wouldn't be having all these problems," I fire back.

"You talk a lot to be as young as you are. I should've let my man smack the tongue out your mouth at the block party!"

Magic roars like the king of the urban jungle, "Both of y'all shut up! Just because you got one hit doesn't mean I won't drop both of you from Magic Music." He whips out his cell phone. "I can call Jay-Z, Beyoncé, 50, Mary J., anybody I want to replace you on Saturday. Now either shut up *right now* or I'm on speed dial, and that's my word!"

It's so quiet in here now you could hear a church mouse spit.

I won't bore you with the details of the three rehearsals we had the week leading up to Summer Fest, but I will say that me and Bang Up spoke to each other only three, maybe four times. Magic banned us from bringing entourages or groupies to any rehearsals or recording sessions before Saturday. He said he was being "egalitarian" with the ban, but all three of us knew he wasn't talking to me. I'm not the insecure one who has to have a bunch of people around me all the time.

◆

On Saturday morning I wake up early because a healthy dose of late summer sun is slow-roasting the tip of my nose. I should be happy with my life, but I'm not. Ever since this hip-hop thing jumped off for real, it's been one drama after another.

I'm sure most people my age would kill to be in my position. I have a number one record, I'm the main act at the biggest concert series in New York, and I've made more money in one summer than most people's parents make in a whole year. Our video is in heavy rotation on MTV, BET, VH1, and every music video outlet on the Web, and at the end of the month our album is shipping gold to Walmart stores across the country. It will be the first time Walmart has entered into an exclusive agreement with a rap release.

But the flip side is that I lost my best friend, I got jumped, I almost got shot by the cops, I'm starting to hate my recording partner, and a picture of me in handcuffs is all over the Internet. The whole country thinks I'm caught up in the drug game, and the feds arrested me because two coke dealers said I was running drugs for them.

When I weigh both sides, I don't think it's worth it,

especially when the best things in my life don't have anything to do with music. I have a mother who raised me and my brothers right and who's stuck by me my whole life, I've developed a relationship with a man I look up to like a father, and my new best friend just so happens to be my future wife.

I have to be at Yankee Stadium at 6:30 p.m. even though we probably won't go onstage until 10 or 11 tonight. I really wish Precious was here with me, but after our apple-picking trip, I didn't even bother to ask. While we were there, I asked her why I never saw her bob her head or dance to any music until we were at Rapfest.

She said, "Because bobbing your head to a song is nodding your approval to its message. So if the message doesn't agree with my worldview, I won't dance to it."

"But you had to hear *something* you thought was hot, or I wasn't doing my job right."

"All of the *music* you played was hot," she said, smiling. "But I've trained myself to listen to the lyrics of a song *before* I groove to it. I don't want to be like those people who convince themselves they're just listening to the beat, only to have the lyrics get stuck in their head and live there forever."

As soon as she said that, it dawned on me who she reminds me of. Moms. I don't know why it took me so long to figure that out. But that's probably why I got so mad at her the first time I went to her house. I had already tangled with Moms on most of the things we were arguing about that day.

Tonight Corey and Devin are my Summer Fest chaperones. We're in a limo Power 97 provided, blasting a preview copy of the album.

When the last song fades out, Corey says, "Do y'all realize this is my unofficial going-away party?"

We get quiet because even though he leaves for Norfolk State tomorrow, none of us thought about it like that. Corey sees that he's dampening the party atmosphere, so he tries to liven it up again. "But this is the way to go out. In a limo, backstage access to all the stars at Summer Fest—"

"And we're rolling with Terror Tory, the most googled person in hip-hop!" Devin says.

He's trying to clown me. I can't let him get away with that.

"Don't forget, *you're* rolling with *me*. So you better act right or I'll send you home to your momma!"

We bust out laughing before Corey gets serious again. "But real talk, fam. It's fitting that it's just the three of us. Tonight marks the end of an era. Three the Hard Way will never be the same again." Three the Hard Way is the name my dad called us once he found out I was a boy.

Devin adds, "From now on when you come home, you'll just be visiting."

Moms always told us that Dad said a man had to leave the house when he turned eighteen. He could go to college or the military or get a job, but he had to go. He felt that the only way a boy properly prepares for manhood is when he knows he has to find his own nest once he reaches legal age. And that's the way Moms raised us.

The solemn silence that fills the limo like smoke is

blown away by a loud *pop!* Corey flips and tries to keep a white geyser shooting from a Martinelli's Sparkling Apple Cider bottle from getting on his sharp new outfit. We grab champagne glasses from the rack above our heads, fill them with bubbly, and get our drink on.

After we polish off the bottle of cider, we pump the album again. But after all this talk about my family, I'm struggling. When I think about the way Moms raised us, it frustrates me that a lot of fans are giving me respect because I got arrested. Nobody knows I'm innocent, and nobody really cares to know. It's much more "real" for people to think I'm slinging dope and making hits at the same time.

Through no fault of my own, my street cred has gone through the roof. And the blogs have been lighting up over this. Anticipation for the album is higher than it already was because I got arrested while I was in the studio recording it. One website has a contest where a person can win $1,000 if they correctly guess which song we were recording when I got picked up. I'm trying to figure out how they can answer that since "Sex Machine" isn't even going to be on the album.

I have to say I'm glad I'm on Magic Music, though. I've heard that some record labels leak it to the press when their rappers get in trouble because it leads to more records sold. Supposedly, label execs call this "cash for a rapper's crash." I don't have to worry about that with Magic because he operates with integrity.

But I'll tell you what's downright depressing. When I read some of the comments on the Web responding to articles about my situation, I see that a lot of people aren't even bothered by a celebrity selling drugs or breaking any laws, for that matter. To these folks, if you're a star and they're a fan of yours, they don't want you to go to jail no matter what you do. Something's wrong with that picture.

As we get closer to Yankee Stadium and I start seeing the crowds, my excitement returns and then bubbles over. Corey is obviously feeling the same way because he spontaneously grabs me and Devin and pulls us into a two-armed headlock. With our freshly cut domes secured firmly under an armpit, Corey kisses each of us on top of the head. Devin and I wrestle free because we're pulling up to the stage door.

Even though the three of us are trying hard to be cool, press photographers from *The Source*, XXL, *Billboard*, and *Vibe* magazines capture us cheesing like the "it crowd" rookies we are. I forget all the drama that was swirling around my head and get sucked into the carnival-like atmosphere.

I've never seen this many people in one place. This year's crowd is supposed to top 57,000. That will be a Summer Fest record.

19

Not only is there press at the backstage entrance, there's also a mob of fans who scream every time a limo pulls up and another star gets out. I sign about twenty autographs before I go inside. I hate to cut it short, but it's impossible to sign every request.

As soon as I'm backstage, I feel like a screaming fan. I'm just too cool to do any screaming. The first person I run into is Heavy D, Mount Vernon's biggest rapper (pun intended). He tells me that he's been bumping "Street Theater" in his convertible in Cali since it first came out. LL Cool J, another Cali transplant, walks up and says the song makes him think about New York when he's in L.A. surrounded by palm trees. They both say it sounds like "that classic New York hip-hop" that they haven't heard in years.

My mind is starting to change now. Getting this type of recognition makes the drama seem worth it.

Magic arranged it so that me and Bang Up would have

separate dressing rooms, but we had to promise there wouldn't be any beef between us. The last thing he wants is breakup rumors circulating and the album isn't even out yet.

My dressing room has a bathroom and a sitting area. Nothing fancy, but it's nice enough. I get Corey and Devin to man the door while I hop in the shower. When I get out, I hear conversation going on in the room. You're not going to believe who I see kicked back, snacking on my Veggie Booties and granola, when I step out of the bathroom. Rihanna and Alicia Keys. They actually stopped by to meet me!

Rihanna asks me if I produce R & B tracks, and Alicia wants me to coproduce a song with her for her next album. She wants that old-school New York boom bap that she'll lace with some of her signature chords. She doesn't know that I'm also classically trained on the piano, but since she's sold thirty million albums and won eleven Grammys, I'll let her play her own chords on the track.

I exchange numbers with both of them. After that I'm so amped I decide to go next door to Bang Up's room just to check him out. Of course he's got his same crew there, plus a few different women.

"Yo, this is crazy, right?" I ask him. I think he's as starstruck as I am.

"Son, this is what it's all about."

We give each other the handshake-hug combo.

"You ready?" he asks me.

"You ready?" I shoot back.

We go back and forth with the "you readys" until we

crack up and slap each other five. It feels much better not having tension between us. I was concerned that we wouldn't be able to hide it once we got onstage.

Our show has a good amount of interaction. We're going to bring back some old-school elements to our performance by battling each other—his rhyming skill versus my deejaying. I'll be using my turntablism to cut up some of the hottest hip-hop lyrics of all time, so he's got his hands full.

I'll give you a quick rundown of everybody I met before we went on for our show: Lil Wayne, Big Daddy Kane, Eminem, Premier and Guru, Usher, Mobb Deep, Lil Jon, Red Alert, Chamillionaire, Common, Mos Def, Jermaine Dupri, Ludacris, Nelly, and Hype Williams. Either I ran into them backstage or they came to my room to meet me. All of the New York stars are telling me that I have what it takes to put New York hip-hop back on top. Now I have work lined up for the next year.

It's still hard to believe that real stars actually like the music I make. Four months ago these people didn't even know I existed, but now it's like I'm part of the club.

Me and Bang Up watch the end of Jay-Z's show before we go on. Watching him rip it is giving me the same jittery feeling I had when we shot the video. It's one thing to have a number one record, it's another thing to be able to perform before 57,000 people and keep them on their feet. Jay-Z has been doing this for years, so he could rock a show with just his classic joints. But we have only one hit and are going to be performing songs from an album that won't even be released for another two weeks.

Magic takes me aside, grabs both of my shoulders, and looks me in the eye. "You heard what everybody's been saying backstage. You have what it takes to put New York back on top. Bang Up is just one rapper, but you're engineering a whole new sound like Teddy Riley did with New Jack Swing and Timbaland did with Dirty South. Don't forget that. Every fan out there wants you to succeed. You understand?"

Magic needs to start coaching or something because that speech has me ready to explode onto the stage. He talks to Bang Up next. I can't hear what he's saying, but Bang Up looks dead serious and keeps nodding his head in agreement.

Jay-Z hugs both of us when he comes offstage. He tells us to rep New York to the fullest.

When we walk onstage, all of Yankee Stadium goes berserk. You haven't heard cheering until you've heard 57,000 people screaming your name. I can feel the applause in my bones, all the way down to my toes. It's no wonder pride gets the best of most stars, because right now I feel like a king.

Bang Up grabs the mike, and I jump on the turntables. He tosses me a question.

"Yo, son, you look a little young. How old are you?"

"I'm sixteen."

"Man, what do you know about hip-hop? You wasn't even born until 1993. You heard of Grandmaster Flash and the Furious Five?"

I bring in "The Message," and the crowd goes nuts. I

let it play while I'm back spinning and scratching on the second turntable, and then Bang Up interrupts.

"Alright, alright, hold up. You know about Flash, but what you know about Boogie Down Productions?"

I put on "South Bronx," and the crowd gets silly hyped.

After that it's a hip-hop call and response. Bang Up calls and I respond.

"Wu-Tang Clan?"

"C.R.E.A.M."

"Tupac?"

"California Love."

"Biggie?"

"Hypnotize."

"DMX?"

"Ruff Ryders' Anthem."

"Dre and Snoop?"

"Still D.R.E."

"T.I.?"

"What You Know."

It's pandemonium by the time we get to the songs of the artists who performed before us tonight. The Bronx is shaking, and we don't have earthquakes in New York.

I bring in the instrumental to "Street Theater" and ask, "This is a beat I made. What you know about that?"

When Bang Up starts spitting the lyrics to "Street Theater," even the stars watching backstage go buck wild. Now that Bang Up is into his verse, my focus shifts. I play the hype man, getting the crowd to stand up and wave their hands in the air while Bang Up is flowing. Yo, we're ripping it crazy right now!

When you're onstage, you can see only one or two rows into the audience because of the bright stage lights. Just after Bang Up finishes the first hook, I see some commotion. The middle of the crowd parts like the Red Sea. I see Boo Boo calmly approaching the stage with that crazy look in his eye. He's packing a heater and pointing it directly at me.

Before I have time to react, he starts firing. I hold up the record that's in my hand and fall backward. I stumble from the platform, and my legs buckle underneath me. I tumble off the back of the stage, which is at least ten feet off the ground. I hear people screaming and more shots being fired as I'm falling.

When I hit the ground, everything goes silent. My whole body is in pain, and I taste blood in my mouth. All of a sudden I start to feel sleepy. I try to fight it off because I don't want to go to sleep until I get to a hospital.

Now I can't see. I can't move. This must have been what Baron felt like. Maybe I should've given the religion stuff more thought. So I say what he said.

"Yo, Jesus, if you're real you can save me."

And that was it.

20

I see myself in my coffin. It's black with red interior. I'm wearing my black suit and the red necktie Mr. Lord bought me, tied in a cross knot. I see Precious, Moms, Devin, Corey, and Mr. and Mrs. Lord in the front row of the church. It's painful to see them crying and hurting so bad. I start to cry too. I don't know where I am right now, but it's hot as hellfire.

Despite the blazing temperature, I wake up in a cold sweat. My heart is beating so fast I can barely breathe. It takes me a few minutes to realize I'm in my bedroom. Devin is sound asleep. We moved Corey's bed out once he went down to Norfolk State three weeks ago.

When I sit up, pain from my bruised tailbone shoots up my back like an electric shock.

Believe it or not, holding up that record when Boo Boo started firing saved my life. And I'm not the only one calling it a miracle. All the doctors at Harlem Hospital said the same thing. A vinyl record isn't supposed to deflect a

.45 caliber bullet shot at you from twenty feet away. The record shattered when one of the bullets hit it, and the fragments that scattered scratched both of my corneas.

I grab my eye drops from the nightstand and put some in my burning eyes.

Other than biting my tongue so hard when I hit the ground that it needed stitches, nothing else on me was seriously hurt. I am glad to be alive, but I'm still in shock. I can't believe that Boo Boo let Yancy and Carl put him up to kill me. After he was arrested, I guess he realized they were just using him to protect themselves, so he told the cops everything. That's what got me off the hook. Yancy and Carl are going to be behind bars for a long time. But the judge cut Boo Boo some slack because of his rough upbringing and his willingness to cooperate. His testimony ended any chance that Yancy and Carl would get a deal. Boo Boo should be out by the time I graduate from high school.

And guess where I'm going to be graduating from? St. Urse. I actually applied myself and aced the entrance exam. I decided to leave South Side because after all that I've been through, I want to be in a place that's going to challenge me to be the best *me* I can possibly be. That's what Corey, Devin, and Precious are doing, and that's what my dad would want me to do. Of course tuition's not a problem now. But one thing I found out *after* I enrolled is that because St. Urse is a parochial school, I'm required to take Bible class.

It seems like the guy in the sky is setting me up again. It started with him surrounding me with all these secret agents, beginning with my moms. Then he sets it up so the only way I can do it big with my music is if I go to church and afterward deliberate with his personal defense attorney, Mr. Lord. Then he drops the Precious bomb and sends the most beautiful agent in the world right to me. She gets me open and takes me to a rap concert with a thugged-out Jesus dude saying scary things about God, the universe, and eternity. And now he has me in a school where I have to read the Bible 180 days a year.

But real talk, I'm seeing that there are a lot of cats in the Bible whose lives were a lot like mine. I never knew that Jesus did his thing in the streets and that he was up in the party with hustlers and crooks. There were also three dudes in the Old Testament hired by a king to make beats. If you think I'm bugging, check out Mark 6:56, Matthew 9:10, and 1 Chronicles 25:6.

I'm also going out for St. Urse's debate team, partly to spend more time in Precious's orbit, but also to develop my own skills. Who knows, I might apply to Harvard next year, and being on the debate team will look good on my application.

Nowadays Moms and I are tighter than ever. Every Friday I take her out to dinner in the city after she gets off work and before I go on the air.

Bang Up and I are about to release our next single, and since Summer Fest we've become what I call "oil-and-water friends." That means we'll probably never completely bond, but we're cool enough to continue recording without killing each other.

Fat Mike moved down to Edison, New Jersey, and

joined the Job Corps. The word on the street is that he's studying culinary arts. Fat Mike the chef. That's not as catchy as Raekwon the chef, but I don't think Fat Mike will have any problem learning his way around a kitchen. The important thing is that he's trying to get his life together.

But you know the wildest thing that's happened in the past five months? Me and the guy in the sky rap now. Don't get me wrong, I'm still not a saint, and I still have a lot of questions, but I figure he knows more than anyone else I can ask, including Mr. Lord. But it's not like the movies where a voice comes out of the sky and gives me answers. I just get greater clarity on things after we rap about it.

The way I see it, if he kept me from getting shot twice in one summer, there has to be a reason why I'm still here. As a matter of fact, I think I'm going to ask him why he put me on this earth. Maybe you should do it too. Then you can shoot me an email and we can compare notes. If I'm in the studio, it might take me awhile to respond, but I'm giving you my word that I'll definitely hit you back. Until then, I'll holler at you later.

Peace,

Terror Tory

P.S. My web address is unchartedterrortory.com.

Acknowledgments

Thanks to Adrienne Ingrum for believing that I could write something other than a screenplay or music video treatment, and for not allowing this idea to die despite its various permutations. Thanks to Andrea Doering for catching the vision and running with it, for your editorial expertise, and for being an All-Pro quarterback. Jessica Miles, you did an excellent job batting cleanup and getting every ounce of story out of me. Nathan, Michele, Cheryl, Twila, Karen, Rod, and the entire team at Baker/Revell, your commitment to this unorthodox novel gave it life beyond my laptop.

Daverne, Mirlee, and Margie, your support and belief in me during the dark days were invaluable. To the Half Dozen, we have been fruitful and multiplied into one shy of two dozen! To Sweetie, my best friend, writing partner, and ultimate teammate, I couldn't have done it without you. Lee, Jean-Angel, Truth, and Justice, collectively you are my greatest creative achievement. I expect you to stand on Mommy's and Daddy's shoulders to see even greater ways to represent the King. To the great I AM, you are the vine and I am a branch. Despite my best efforts of mutiny, you led me into the wilderness and showed me that apart from you, I can do nothing.

Booker T. Mattison is an author and filmmaker who wrote the screenplay for and directed the film adaptation of Zora Neale Hurston's *The Gilded Six Bits*, which aired on Showtime. His films have been screened at the Smithsonian Institute, the Library of Congress, the Directors Guild of America, and Harvard University. He has written and directed music videos that have aired on BET, MTV Europe, and the Gospel Music Channel.

Mattison has taught literary criticism at the College of New Rochelle and film production at Brooklyn College. He received his master of fine arts in film from New York University and his bachelor of science in mass communication from Norfolk State University.

He lives in New York with his wife and four children.